COMMON SENSE AND FOWLS

COMMON SENSE AND FOWLS

JANE CUTLER

PICTURES BY LYNNE BARASCH

Farrar Straus Giroux   New York

Distributed in Canada by Douglas & McIntyre Publishing Group
Printed in the United States of America
Designed by Robbin Gourley
First edition, 2005
1 3 5 7 9 10 8 6 4 2

www.fsgkidsbooks.com

Library of Congress Cataloging-in-Publication Data
Cutler, Jane.
Common sense and fowls / Jane Cutler ; pictures by
Lynne Barasch.— 1st ed.
p.   cm.
Summary: When a group of their neighbors plans to oust
Mrs. Krnc because she feeds the pigeons that cause a mess,
Rachel and her great-uncle Benson work to encourage better
communication and search for an alternate solution.
ISBN-13: 978-0-374-32262-5
ISBN-10: 0-374-32262-7
[1. Interpersonal relations—Fiction.   2. Neighbors—Fiction.
3. Communication—Fiction.   4. Great-uncles—Fiction.
5. Pigeons—Fiction.   6. Birds—Fiction.]   I. Barasch, Lynne, ill.
II. Title.

PZ7.C985Co   2005
[Fic]—dc22

2004047189

For Tom Parker

COMMON SENSE AND FOWLS

1

Rachel was in the driveway Friday after school practicing free throws and layups when her across-the-street neighbor Brian Bishop turned up.

"Hi, Rachel," Brian said.

Rachel shot and missed. "You missed," Brian noted.

"Thanks, Brian," Rachel said.

"What for?" he asked.

"For breaking my concentration."

"I didn't break your concentration, Rachel," Brian said.

"You talked."

"I didn't talk, Rachel."

"Did," said Rachel, dribbling and getting ready to take another shot.

"Didn't!" said Brian. He rushed her and grabbed the ball.

"You can't do that, Brian! Give it back."

Brian bounced the ball to Rachel. "All I said was 'Hi,' " he said. "That's not talking."

"It's not? What is it, then?"

"Let me have a turn, Rachel," he said, "please?"

Rachel sighed and gave Brian the ball. He heaved it underhanded in the direction of the basket. But it fell short and rolled into the bushes.

"Guess what, Rachel," Brian said as he went to get the ball.

"What?"

"I'm a Reluctant Reader."

"I know you're a reluctant reader, Brian," said Rachel. "That's not news. You're in second grade, and you can hardly read a thing."

"It is news, Rachel," Brian said. "It's official now."

"Official?"

"Yep. My mom and I had a meeting at school today with Mr. Henderson and Ms. Stone, and it's official. I'm a Reluctant Reader. Big *R*, big *R*. My reading is Delayed. I might even be Learning-Challenged. I have to spend part of every day in a Special Ed class with Ms. Stone. And Mr. Henderson wants Mom to get me a tutor for my reading. That's how far behind I am!"

Rachel had never heard Brian sound so happy about anything that had to do with school.

"You had a meeting with the principal and the special ed teacher and you need a tutor because you're having trouble learning to read—"

"And learning other stuff, too!" Brian interrupted cheerfully.

"And you're sounding like it's your birthday or something." Brian tossed her the ball, and Rachel bounced it thoughtfully from one hand to the other. "I don't get it, Brian."

Brian shrugged and grinned. "Me neither, Rachel. I don't get hardly anything."

Rachel and Brian listened to the ball bouncing. Then Rachel took a few shots—perfect shots—while Brian watched.

"Do you think Uncle Benson could be my tutor?" Brian asked finally. "Mom's going to call him."

"I don't know, Brian," Rachel said. Everybody wanted Rachel's Great-Uncle Benson to be their tutor. He had more kids to teach than any other tutor in the district. "He's really busy."

"I know," said Brian. Then he smiled. "But he'll say yes. Uncle Benson would never not be *my* tutor."

Rachel took a careful shot from about the free-throw line. Swish. Perfect.

She knew Brian was right. Of course Uncle Benson would say yes. Brian was around so much, he was like one of the family. And Uncle Benson couldn't even bring himself to say no to total strangers, so how could he say no to somebody who was almost family?

"Right, Rachel?" Brian prompted.

"Right, Brian," Rachel agreed.

Rachel put the ball away. "I have to go over to Mr. Twiddle's store to get Molly," she said, picking up the dog's leash from where she'd left it on the ground. "Want to come with me?"

"Sure," said Brian.

Rachel and Brian started off. As they walked to Mr. Twiddle's store, Rachel told Brian she'd gotten a postcard from her old sitter, Mrs. T., who'd retired and moved to Washington State to live with her sister.

"I miss Mrs. T.," Brian said.

"I do, too," said Rachel. "Sometimes I do, anyway. But I don't need a sitter anymore, so it's probably good that she retired."

Twiddle's Fine Foods / The Uncommon Market stood at the top of a hill. And from half a block away, they could see the white buckets filled with bunches of colorful flowers on the sidewalk out in front. They could see the sturdy wooden stands holding cartons filled with all different kinds of vegetables and fruits.

They could see old Molly, dozing underneath the stands. And they could see tall Mr. Twiddle in his baseball cap and Mr. Twiddle's short assistant, Ling, wearing her dark green apron, standing out in front of the store. They were gazing down the hill in the direction of Elm Avenue, where two of the neighborhood's most unusual people, Mr. Gregory Gioia (Joy-a) and Mrs. Ksenja Krnc (K-sen-ya Krents), lived. Mr. Twiddle and Ling seemed very interested in whatever they were looking at.

Rachel and Brian hurried up so they could find out what it was.

"Hi, Mr. Twiddle!" Rachel called. "Hi, Ling!"

Mr. Twiddle waved without turning around.

Ling turned. She smiled her friendly big smile. "Hi, Rachel!" she called. "Hi, Brian!" Then she went back to watching.

Rachel and Brian ran the rest of the way up the hill.

"What are you guys looking at?" Rachel asked.

"She's at it again," said Mr. Twiddle, his voice full of concern.

Rachel and Brian looked down the hill. Brian breathed in. "The pigeon lady," he said.

"Yep, here we go again," said Mr. Twiddle, all doom and gloom, shaking his head as he turned to go inside. "Mark my words," he warned, "Mr. Gioia's not going to be happy about this. I'd say trouble's coming."

Rachel remembered something Uncle Benson said. "Try not to trouble trouble until trouble troubles you, Mr. Twiddle," she quoted.

Mr. Twiddle looked reproachfully at her. Then he went inside his store.

It always works better when Uncle Benson says stuff like that, Rachel thought. She looked back downhill.

Mrs. Krnc, the pigeon lady, was out on the sidewalk in front of her house, the only neglected house on the block. She was flinging stale bread out of a paper sack, and all around her were pigeons.

What a sight the old woman was, with her ancient, colorless sweater buttoned all the way up to her chin and her pink socks sagging down around her worn brown shoes; with her matted hair covered, as it always was, by a faded cotton kerchief.

The pushy pigeons crowded around her feet. They roosted on the railings of her dilapidated porch and on her sagging roof. They pecked around on her dried-up lawn and on her cracked front walk.

Pigeons paraded on the public sidewalk in front of her house and spilled over the curb and down the gutter and right out into the middle of the street. They perched on the power lines that stretched overhead.

Even worse, the pigeons made themselves at home on all the neighbors' well-kept houses and nicely tended lawns and gardens. They perched on the neighbors' neat porches, on their perfect roofs and gates and fences, and sat on their shiny cars. And every single place there were pigeons, there were pigeon droppings. Pigeon droppings were all over the place.

When the bag of bread was empty, the pigeon lady went back into her house. She closed the rickety front door carefully so none of the birds could come inside.

By the time Uncle Benson rode up on his bright green, twenty-one-speed mountain bike, Ling had gone back to work, too, and Rachel and Brian were about to start home with Molly on her leash.

Uncle Benson's bike saddlebags were overflowing with books and papers, and he was more than a little out of breath.

"Uncle Benson, guess what?" called Brian, dancing excitedly up to him. "I'm Challenged!"

"So am I, Brian!" said Uncle Benson, chuckling so his fat belly shook. He took off his red-and-white plastic racing helmet, wiped his sweaty face with his

red bandanna handkerchief, and took a long drink from his water bottle.

"Tired, Uncle Benson?" asked Rachel.

"A little," he said. "It would be nice to have all my students in one place. It's the riding around from place to place that wears me out. I'm beginning to think I should have kept my motorcycle instead of getting a bike."

Rachel remembered how happy she'd been when she found out Uncle Benson had replaced the motorcycle he'd bought to travel around the country on with a bicycle. That was when she knew for sure his visit to her family wasn't going to end and her wish was going to come true: Uncle Benson was going to stay with them forever.

"Maybe you need to get a motorcycle again," she said.

"Maybe you need to get a car," Brian suggested.

Just then Mr. Twiddle and Ling came back outside to see Uncle Benson. "Hey," Mr. Twiddle said.

"Hey, Mr. Twiddle," Uncle Benson replied.

"Well," said Mr. Twiddle, pulling an especially long face, "she's at it again." He nodded in the direction of the pigeon lady's house.

"I can see that," said Uncle Benson, "and after all the fuss Mr. Gioia made the other times."

"Yep," said Mr. Twiddle, nodding grimly.

Uncle Benson closed his water bottle and put it away.

"Trouble's coming," warned Mr. Twiddle.

"Now, Mr. Twiddle," said Uncle Benson, "try not to trouble trouble until trouble troubles you!"

Mr. Twiddle looked reproachfully at him.

"I already tried that one, Uncle Benson," Rachel said.

"Mrs. Krnc loves the pigeons," Ling said. "They are her only friends."

"It's true," said Uncle Benson. "But I guess she's forgotten how angry Mr. Gioia gets about the mess all those fowls leave."

"Fowls?" asked Brian.

"Another word for birds," replied Uncle Benson.

"Wait until Mr. Gioia gets home," Mr. Twiddle said. "Mr. Gioia thought he and Mrs. Krnc had come to an understanding about no more pigeon feeding after the last time. He won't be happy about this."

"Just like he wasn't happy about the library changing its hours or the town putting in more parking meters downtown. He's found a lot to be unhappy about since he retired," observed Ling.

———

"Mrs. Krnc and Mr. Gioia," said Rachel, as she and Brian and Molly and Uncle Benson walked home. "That's kind of funny, isn't it, Uncle Benson?"

"What's funny, Rachel?" Brian wanted to know.

"Their names are funny. The pigeon lady's name is all consonants. And Mr. Gioia's name is almost all vowels. And they're neighbors and . . ." Rachel wasn't sure what, exactly, she was trying to say. "It just strikes me as being funny."

"Funny ha-ha?" asked Brian doubtfully.

"No," said Rachel, "funny strange."

"Oh," said Brian. He thought for a minute. "Now I get it," he fibbed. "The pigeon lady has common sense and her neighbor has fowls," he said. "Yup. *Strange*."

Rachel stopped walking to stare at Brian. "Brian," she said, "that's the worst joke I've ever heard."

"Joke?" Brian said.

"Joke. That joke you just made."

"I didn't make a joke," said Brian. "What are you talking about?"

Uncle Benson started to laugh. First his belly shook, then tears filled his eyes. "You two," he said. "If vaudeville weren't dead, we could take your show on the road. You'd be a hit!"

"Vaudeville's dead?" asked Brian, looking concerned. "When did vaudeville die? What's vaudeville?"

"Time for you to go to your own house now, Brian," Rachel said firmly when they got home. "I'll see you tomorrow."

Brian hesitated. "Vaudeville?" he said.

"Tomorrow," said Rachel.

"Died?" Brian said.

Uncle Benson unpacked his bike bags. Rachel took off Molly's leash and shoved her into the backyard.

"Tomorrow," said Rachel.

"Um . . ." said Brian.

Rachel put her hands on her hips. "Brian," she warned.

"Bye, Rachel. Bye, Uncle Benson," Brian decided. Off he went.

"Brian forgot to tell you," Rachel said, as she helped Uncle Benson carry his stuff into the house, "his mom's going to call you. He's officially a reluctant reader now. He needs a tutor."

"Ah," said Uncle Benson.

"Will you tutor him, Uncle Benson?"

"Of course I'll tutor Brian, Rachel," said Uncle Benson. "It'll be my pleasure and my privilege to tutor Brian." He thought for a moment. "And I know exactly where I'll start with this particular reluctant reader, too."

"Where will you start?" Rachel wanted to know.

"I bet you can guess," said Uncle Benson.

"Just tell me, Uncle Benson."

"I'll start with common sense and fowls, of course."

Rachel shook her head. "Uncle Benson, that is still the worst joke I've ever heard," she said.

2

Later, when Mrs. Krnc's neighbor
Mr. Gioia came home, he saw the pigeon droppings.
Up the hill he roared to the ten-minute customer
parking spot in front of Twiddle's Fine Foods. There
he carefully parked his fancy sports car.

Then, out of the trunk, he got a large tarp and
some rope. He covered the car with the tarp and se-
cured the tarp with rope.

Mr. Twiddle watched from the doorway of his
shop.

"Hey," said Mr. Twiddle, when Mr. Gioia had finished turning his car into what looked like an extremely large parcel ready to be mailed.

Mr. Gioia stood facing away from Mr. Twiddle.
His sunglasses were pushed up on top of his head, the
sleeves of his Windbreaker were pushed up above his

elbows, and his hands were stuck into the back pockets of his neatly pressed jeans. He gazed down the hill. "Pigeons, Mr. Twiddle," he said without turning around, "again!" He made a circle with one of his long arms to show Mr. Twiddle that pigeons had been all over the place.

Mr. Twiddle had to speak to Mr. Gioia's back. "Yes," he agreed.

"And I thought we had an agreement, Mrs. Krnc and I," Mr. Gioia said.

"Yes, yes," agreed Mr. Twiddle.

Shaking his head, Mr. Gioia started down the hill.

"Ten minutes," Mr. Twiddle called timidly, "Mr. Gioia?"

"Mr. Twiddle?" said Mr. Gioia, turning back.

"Parking?" Mr. Twiddle reminded him. "In the green zone? In front of the store?"

"Thanks, neighbor," Mr. Gioia warmly replied. He waved. "I appreciate your help. I'm sure you won't mind my parking there until this pigeon problem is cleared up once and for all. Can't have my car getting dirty."

Mr. Gioia lost no time getting organized.

By the next morning, Saturday, he'd slipped flyers

17

under every door on his block except Mrs. Krnc's and left a stack of them at Twiddle's Fine Foods.

The flyers said:

PIGEON LADY STRIKES AGAIN!
Our neighbor Mrs. Krnc has broken her promise.
How can we protect ourselves?
Come to the block meeting today, 3 p.m.,
748 Elm Ave.,
to decide.
Sincerely,
Your neighbor, Gregory G. Gioia

Lesley, Rachel's older sister, steamed into the house at noon carrying several of the flyers. "Take a look at these!" she said.

"Lesley, you don't have to shout," said her brother, Jonathan, who was doing his math homework at the dining room table and eating a black bean and brown rice and white cheese and green chile burrito he'd just made himself for lunch.

"Am I shouting?" yelled his sister.

"You are!" said her mom, who was on her way to meet her friend Bernice for their Saturday run.

"Well, if I am, there's a reason," said Lesley.

"What's the reason this time?" asked her dad, not

looking up from the baseball game he was watching on TV in the living room.

"Yeah, Lesley," said Rachel, coming out of the kitchen, where she'd been checking out the contents of the refrigerator, trying to decide what to fix herself for lunch, "what's up?"

"Well," said Lesley, "I have a feeling something unjust may be in the works. Look at this flyer."

"I'll look at it when I get back," said her mom as she left.

"I will, after the game," her dad called from the other room.

"When I finish eating," Jonathan said. "I don't want my burrito to get cold."

"Doesn't anyone in this family care about justice?" asked Lesley, putting the flyers down on the dining table.

"I do, Lesley," said Rachel. "Let me see." She sat down to read. Lesley stood over her. "Where's Uncle Benson, Rachel?" Lesley asked.

Rachel rolled her eyes at her sister. "Lesley," she said, "I'm reading."

"Yeah, Lester," said Jonathan, "she's reading about injustice. Let her read."

"All I said was—"

"He's over at the Bishops'," Rachel said. "He's talking to Brian's mom about helping Brian with *his* reading. Brian's a reluctant reader. Uncle Benson's going to tutor him."

Lesley sighed. "A reluctant reader. Like everyone in this family. Maybe Uncle Benson needs to tutor everybody!"

"Shhh," said Rachel. She finished reading. "I don't understand what you're worried about, Lesley," she began.

"That's why I need to see Uncle Benson," said Lesley, who got frustrated easily. "I can't stand around all day while everybody does everything in the world except concern themselves with justice!"

"I'm not doing anything except concern myself with justice," Rachel objected. "I just said, 'I don't understand—' "

"I know that, Rachel," said her sister.

"So now you're supposed to explain," Rachel prompted.

"I don't have time," said Lesley.

"How come?" Jonathan wanted to know.

"Because I'm afraid that every minute I stand here doing nothing, injustice may be getting ahead of me."

"It's not *just* not to explain things to people,"

teased Jonathan. "Justice is never served by keeping people ignorant."

"Right," said Rachel, starting back to the kitchen. "If I'm ignorant, I don't have any idea what's going on. I don't know whether something is just or unjust. I can't even have an opinion. You're missing an opportunity here, Lesley. You could educate me. But since you don't want to take the time, I'm going to make myself something to eat."

Rachel returned to her cooking.

Lesley stood by the dining room table until Jonathan finished the last bite of his burrito. Then she pushed the flyer under his nose, crossed her arms, and waited.

Jonathan began to read, leaning back and looking only mildly interested. Then he leaned forward. Finally he stood up and called, "Rachel, where's Uncle Benson?"

Rachel came out of the kitchen. She had a frying pan in one hand and an avocado in the other. "I already said, he's over at the Bishops'. Why?"

"Lesley's right. He ought to take a look at this."

"Why?"

"Well, in case things get out of hand."

"What things?

"Things at the meeting."

"Why do you think they might get out of hand?"

Jonathan held up the flyer. "There's something about this that doesn't feel right to me," Jonathan explained.

"That's what I meant," said Lesley.

"Like what?" Rachel wanted to know.

"Having a meeting to talk about a neighbor without that neighbor there feels wrong," Jonathan said.

"There could be a hidden agenda!" declared Lesley.

"What's that?"

"Lesley's afraid that the meeting will be about more than this flyer says it's going to be about," Jonathan explained. "Mr. Gioia was really angry the last time Mrs. Krnc did this. And now he thinks she's broken a promise. And he's gathering all the neighbors together to talk about her—something about that bothers us."

"Jon," Lesley said, "we're wasting time."

"We'll be back soon, Rach," Jonathan promised.

Rachel went into the kitchen.

She put a flour tortilla into the preheated oven and sprinkled water on it, to make it soft, the way Uncle Benson had shown her. While the tortilla was heating, she warmed some brown rice and black beans in the frying pan. She grated a bit of cheese and chopped up half of a tomato and part of the avocado.

When the tortilla was ready, she sprinkled it with cheese, and when the cheese melted, she transferred the tortilla to a large plate, filled it with rice and beans, tomato and avocado, topped it all with some green chile sauce, and rolled it up tight, carefully tucking in the ends so none of the filling would spill out.

Then she carried it into the dining room, where Jonathan had left his dirty plate and glass, his math homework, and the rest of the flyers.

Rachel sat down at a clean space and picked one up. She took a bite of her burrito and began to read the flyer again.

When she'd finished eating and reading, she went into the living room and sat on the arm of her father's chair.

"How's the game?" she asked.

"Not very exciting so far," he answered.

"It'll probably get better," she said.

"Where there's life, there's hope," he agreed.

"Dad, I don't understand this," she said.

"Don't understand what?" her father replied, not taking his eyes off the TV screen.

"This flyer that Lesley brought home. The one she's been fussing about."

"Doesn't take much to make your sister fuss."

"Jonathan, too," said Rachel.

"Jonathan, too? Well, in that case, I'll take a look."

Rachel's dad read the flyer quickly and handed it back to her with a smile. "Not complicated," he told her. "I'd say it's about pigeon droppings in the vicinity of Mr. Gioia's property and his car." He turned his attention back to the game.

Rachel looked at the flyer again. "But, Dad," she said, "Lesley and Jonathan thought there might be a hidden agenda. What's an agenda?"

Rachel's father's favorite team had men on second and third and only one out. "Pigeon droppings on houses and cars is what it's about," he assured her, his eyes glued to the TV. "You can look up *agenda* in the dictionary. Now let's watch the game."

Rachel wasn't as interested in the game as she was in the pigeon problem. She decided to head over to the Bishops', too.

3

Just as Rachel was about to leave, Lesley, Jonathan, and Uncle Benson came back. Brian tagged along behind them. When he saw Rachel, he zoomed up the steps in front of the others. "Uncle Benson's my tutor!" he said.

"That's great, Brian," Rachel said. "Now hush so I can hear what they're talking about."

"They're talking about the pigeon lady," Brian said.

"We're talking about Mrs. Krnc," said Uncle Benson.

"And about the meeting Mr. Gioia's called," Jonathan said.

"And the possibility of a hidden agenda," said Lesley.

Uncle Benson hadn't had lunch yet, and he went into the kitchen to fix himself a quick bite.

"You don't have much time, Uncle Benson," Lesley warned. "The meeting begins at three."

"Can I come?" Brian wanted to know.

"If it's okay with your mom," Uncle Benson said.

Brian went back home to find out.

Uncle Benson drank a glass of apple juice and quickly ate a small cheese and honey mustard sandwich. "Let's get ready," he said. "Somebody take a pen and paper, in case we want to write things down."

Jonathan and Lesley both went to get pens and paper.

"Uncle Benson," said Rachel, "what does *agenda* mean?"

"Rachel, look it up," Rachel's father called from the living room.

How does he do that? Rachel wondered.

"I don't have time, Dad," she called back. "We're leaving."

Rachel and Uncle Benson went out front to wait for Lesley and Jonathan. Brian was already there, sitting on the steps with his elbows on his knees and his chin in his hands, staring into space.

"What are you thinking about, Brian?" Rachel wanted to know.

"Nothing," Brian said.

Rachel was jealous. She remembered how it felt to be a little kid who could sit on the steps and think about nothing.

From down the block on Elm Avenue, Rachel could see that people on their way to the meeting at Mr. Gioia's had stopped near the pigeon lady's house and were standing around, talking. Most of the pigeon lady's closest neighbors were on hand. Like tour guides at a national park, they were showing people who lived on other streets all the damage the pigeons had done.

Rachel, Lesley, Jonathan, Brian, and Uncle Benson stopped, too. "What a mess!" Jonathan observed.

"Jonathan, you traitor!" exclaimed Lesley.

"I'm not a traitor!" Jonathan protested. "I'm honest! It's a mess!"

"It is, Lesley," Rachel said. "You have to admit it."

"Well, that's not the point, anyway," said Lesley.

"What is the point?" Rachel asked. "I thought the mess the pigeons are making was the point."

"The point is," Uncle Benson said, "that we don't know anything until we get to the meeting and listen to what people have to say and find out what's on their minds. Some people may have one point, and some may have another. We'll find out when we get there.

"What's more, we'll experience democracy in action! Why, we'll all learn more today than we could learn in a year of history or political science or civics classes!"

Uncle Benson's eyes were shining. "This reminds me of something my old friend Horatio told me about education," he said.

"Horatio told you something about education?" said Rachel.

"He did," said Uncle Benson. "It was a long time ago when I was just a teacher in training and Horatio was the Head Teacher at the Raisin' Brain School for Growing Girls and Boys."

"He was growing girls and boys?" asked Brian.

"Of course not, Brian," said Jonathan. "The boys and girls at the school were growing."

"Bigger?" asked Brian.

"Smarter," said Jonathan.

"Well, smarter and bigger both, probably, right, Uncle Benson?" said Rachel.

"As I was saying," Uncle Benson said, "you know what Horatio said about education . . ."

"No, Uncle Benson," Rachel said. "What *did* Horatio say about education?" She knew Uncle Benson needed a straight guy any time he told a story about Horatio.

"You may find this hard to believe, Rachel, coming from a man like Horatio, who was, after all, a Master Teacher of Teachers as well as a Master Teacher of Teachers of Teachers—"

"Uncle Benson," Rachel interrupted.

"Yes, Rachel?"

"Go on to the part about what Horatio said about education."

"Oh, right," said Uncle Benson. "What Horatio, the Master Teacher, said about education was, '*Experience* is the best teacher!' "

"Uncle Benson," said Rachel, "that's not funny!"

"I think it is," said Uncle Benson, wiping tears of laughter from his eyes.

"I think it is, too," said Brian, looking confused and loyal at the same time.

"Anyway," said Uncle Benson, "it's what we're going to do right now. We're going to *experience* democracy. We're going to learn about it firsthand. Horatio would be proud."

"Look, Rachel, there's your mom," said Brian.

Rachel's mom and her friend Bernice were standing together on the sidewalk near the pigeon lady's house.

Lesley and Jonathan said hi to their mother and her friend and kept walking. Rachel and Uncle Benson, with Brian hanging on, stopped to chat.

"That woman really is a troublemaker," Bernice said.

"Are you coming to the meeting?" Uncle Benson asked.

"Maybe. After I get cleaned up. I'm all sweaty from our jog," said Bernice.

"I'm not. I'm going home," said Rachel's mom. "But somebody has got to do something about this. What a mess. I'm sure glad we don't live over here, aren't you?"

"We're going to the meeting, Mom," said Rachel. "We're going to listen to the discussion so we can understand what's going on."

"I don't think there's anything to discuss," said Bernice. "This has got to stop!" She gave Rachel's mom a hug and went off toward her own house.

"I have to go, too," Rachel's mother said. "Hope the meeting is interesting."

When Rachel glanced at the pigeon lady's front window, she saw that the ragged curtain was pulled aside and the pigeon lady was peering out. She looked just like a witch in a fairy tale, but like a frightened witch.

Then Rachel saw a small, extremely old man dressed unseasonably in a long, black coat coming toward the pigeon lady's house. Aided by a stout cane, he advanced with surprising speed. And when he got to the walkway that led to Mrs. Krnc's, he rested both hands on the cane and stood, like a sentry on duty, glaring all about from beneath fierce white eyebrows.

"Who in the world is that?" Rachel asked.

"Wow!" said Brian. "I bet that's the oldest man in the world!"

"I believe that's Mr. Damesek, the housepainter," said Uncle Benson, regarding the man thoughtfully. "The retired housepainter, I should say. Hardly ever leaves his apartment anymore . . ."

"What's he doing out of his apartment now?" asked Brian.

"I'm not sure," said Uncle Benson. "But there is a story about him that might give us a clue . . ."

"What story?" asked Rachel.

"He's the man who painted the bird mural over at the library years and years ago," said Uncle Benson. "They hired him to paint the inside of the building, and the next thing anybody knew, he'd painted that mural of flying birds on one of the walls."

"I drew some stuff on a wall once," Brian said. "My mom was mad."

"The way I heard the story, he wanted to paint over it with plain paint," Uncle Benson continued, "but everybody liked the bird mural so much, they wouldn't let him."

"Birds," Rachel mused. "He painted birds. And now he's so old, he hardly ever goes out. Except he's here, standing guard at the pigeon lady's house. So this has got to be about birds. Right, Uncle Benson?"

Uncle Benson looked at the small figure whose black coat fell almost to the ground. He nodded. "I think it may be, Rachel," he said.

"What? What about birds? What are you talking about?" said Brian.

"How do you think he found out what was going on?" Rachel asked.

"Well, I know he gets his groceries delivered from Twiddle's. Maybe Mr. Twiddle told him."

"Let's go," Brian nagged. "We're going to miss the whole meeting. He's just standing there. We don't have to watch him stand."

"A couple of minutes ago you were so interested in seeing one of the oldest men in the world," Rachel said.

"Well, I'm not interested now," Brian said. "Come on."

4

Mr. Gioia's living room and his dining room were full of people. All his chairs and sofas were full, and the extra folding chairs he'd set up were, too. Rachel, Brian, Lesley, Jonathan, and Uncle Benson sat on the stairs. From there they could see Mr. Gioia, in the living room, in front of the group.

Mr. Gioia's gold watch gleamed on his wrist, and he looked at it often. He was not a person who would start a meeting even a minute late. At exactly three o'clock, he called for order.

"As you all know," said Mr. Gioia, "we've come together today to address a recurrent problem. Mrs. Krnc is feeding pigeons again. Let me remind you that when she first began to do this, I spoke to her and explained that she had to stop, because of the mess, et cetera. I was sure she understood, and she did agree to stop. But the next thing I knew, there she was, feeding them again.

"It was at that time that I took a poll of the Elm Avenue neighbors, and I found that everybody felt the way I did. So I went back to Mrs. Krnc and I made it very clear to her that I was speaking to her not only for myself, but also for others. I told her she simply had to stop. I used easy words and many gestures. I am sure she understood. Again, she agreed to stop feeding pigeons. And again she has not stuck to her promise." He paused.

"I want to hear your comments and suggestions. Oh, and would someone keep minutes of the meeting?"

"I will," said a woman.

"Thanks," said Mr. Gioia. "Now, who has something to say?"

A small woman with frizzy hair got to her feet. "I think Mrs. Krnc is selfish," she said. "She doesn't care about our property or about how we feel, or she wouldn't be doing this again!"

Several people clapped. The woman sat down.

Mr. Gioia said, "Mary O'Neil suggests that Mrs. Krnc is selfish and doesn't care about the rights or property of others. Anyone else?"

"The lady doesn't understand democracy!" cried

an angry woman. "Most of us on Elm Avenue—in fact, *all* the rest of us on Elm Avenue—have made it clear that we do *not* want pigeon-feeding going on. And in a democracy, the majority rules. But she just goes ahead and does it anyway. She doesn't understand how things are supposed to work."

Mr. Gioia looked at the woman who was taking notes. "Got that?" he asked. "Doesn't understand democracy."

"Wait a minute!" cried Lesley. "What about *minority* rights? In a democracy, the rights of the minority are supposed to be protected. And the rights of the individual, too!"

"Ah," said Mr. Gioia.

"Are you going to write that down?" said Lesley.

"Of course we are," he answered.

"Weren't you going to call the County Health Department last time this happened, Greg?" somebody called out.

"I did," Mr. Gioia said.

"Well, what did they say?"

"They said that flocks of pigeons could create a danger to health," replied Mr. Gioia.

"Mr. Gioia's done his homework," Uncle Benson whispered to Rachel.

A man standing in the back of the dining room

spoke up. "The way I see it is this," he drawled, "the old gal needs those birds because she can't communicate with anybody else. She seems to understand some, but doesn't hardly speak a word of English outside of yes and no. Now, if she did, she'd be able to talk to folks, make friends. She wouldn't need a bunch of mangy birds for friends. What we've got here is a communication problem."

"That's really true," someone agreed. "I tried to talk to her once. No English, that's for sure. And the language she was speaking? Sounded like it was all *z*'s and *x*'s. Not a vowel in sight! Now, if the lady had vowels, maybe we could get someplace with her."

"That's the answer," another man joked. "What Mrs. Krnc needs is vowels—that would take care of the problem!"

"Ah—ha-ha," fake-laughed Mr. Gioia. "Well then, now that we've let off a little steam, where are we with this? Anyone?"

Silence.

"You take it from here, Greg," someone said.

Mr. Gioia cleared his throat. "All right, then," he said. "We all agree, it seems to me, that we've got a big problem: a selfish and maybe even slightly crazy old person who is impossible to communicate with is destroying our property and could be harming our health. It seems to me we have no choice but to take action. Right so far?"

"Right!" said many people.

"Wait a minute!" said Lesley.

"Hold on!" said Jonathan.

Mr. Gioia looked at them. He waited.

"Who's going to speak for the pigeon lady?" Lesley asked.

Mr. Gioia looked around the room. "The young lady wants to know who will speak for the pigeon lady."

"I will," said a woman sitting on the sofa.

"Yes?" said Mr. Gioia.

"Well, when her husband was alive, even though they neglected their property and kept to themselves, she didn't do this."

"True," Mr. Gioia agreed. "But her husband isn't alive now, right?"

"Well, yes," the woman said.

"And now she *is* doing it," he continued.

"Well, yes," the woman said. "All I meant was, she must be lonely."

"I think you're right," said Mr. Gioia. "And the plan I'm about to propose will solve that problem as well as our pigeon problem. As I was saying," he continued, "we have to find a way to take action. And I don't think it will be hard.

"First, we work with the Health Department and the Department of Social Services to gather the evidence we'll need. Then we go to court and prove to a judge that she is too old and addled to live by herself. Then the court will appoint someone to be her guardian and take care of her and her affairs.

"Then we—or whoever becomes her guardian—sell her house to someone who will *not* feed pigeons, and use the money from the sale of the house to pay for her to live in a nice home for old people, where she'll be looked after until she dies. And where she'll have plenty of company and won't be lonely." Mr. Gioia smiled at the group.

"No more pigeon lady. No more pigeons. No more problem!" he said. "It couldn't be simpler! Let's take a vote. All in favor?"

There was a chorus of "Ayes!"

"Opposed?"

Lesley and Jonathan called out, "Nay!"

"Abstain?"

Uncle Benson raised his hand.

"What's that mean?" Brian asked.

"Means he's not voting yes *or* no," Rachel explained.

"The 'ayes' have it," said Mr. Gioia. "Whoever is willing to serve on the committee with me to see this through, please come forward. We'll keep the rest of you posted as to our progress. Thanks to all of you for coming."

Several people went up to the desk to volunteer for the committee. The rest drifted off, talking together. Everyone seemed much happier—except Lesley and Jonathan.

"Uncle Benson," said Lesley after they got outside, "what in the world are we going to do?"

"I know what I'm going to do!" declared Jonathan. "I'm going to teach Mrs. Krnc to speak English!"

"I don't know whether there is anything we can do," said Uncle Benson to Lesley. "I need some time to think."

To Jonathan he said, "That might not be a very practical solution, Jon. Mrs. Krnc has lived in this country for years, and she hasn't chosen to learn English."

"She might change her mind about that now," Jonathan replied.

"She might," said Uncle Benson. "But even if she

did, there really isn't time to teach her enough English to head this off. We'll have to come up with something else."

"Like what, Uncle Benson?" asked Rachel.

"Yeah, like what?" Brian parroted.

"I don't know," Uncle Benson repeated.

They walked home in silence, past the pigeon lady's house, where nobody was creating a disturbance and nobody was standing guard, either.

None of them had ever heard Uncle Benson sound quite so stumped. None of them had ever seen Uncle Benson without an idea when he needed one.

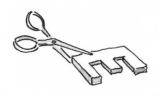

5

When they got home, everybody seemed to want to be alone. Jonathan hit the books. Lesley went to her room to call up her friend Luz and tell her about the meeting. Uncle Benson went into the kitchen and started chopping vegetables for dinner. He always found it easier to think when he was cooking.

Rachel's mom and dad were out. They'd left a note on the kitchen counter saying they'd gone to a movie and would be home later.

"Don't you have to go home, Brian?" Rachel asked.

"Yes," said Brian.

"Soon?"

Brian shrugged.

"Like, now?"

"I want to tell you something first, Rachel."

"What?"

"*I* have an idea."

"You do?"

"Mmm-hmmm."

"About what?"

"The pigeon lady."

"What about her?"

"About how we can help her."

"How?"

Brian stood very close to Rachel. "We can bring her some *vowels*!" he whispered.

"Bring her some vowels?"

Brian shook his head and smiled. "Vowels!" he repeated. "Remember that man said if she could—um—communicate, she would have friends and then she wouldn't need to have pigeons for friends and then the other man said she didn't have any vowels and that's why she couldn't—um—communicate? Remember, Rachel?"

Rachel sighed. "I remember, Brian."

"Well, Uncle Benson just got through explaining to me about vowels, Rachel. When he was over at my house this morning. Vowels are *A, E, I*—"

Rachel interrupted him. "I know about vowels, Brian. What are you getting at?"

"That's what I'm getting at, Rachel. I already told

45

you. If we give the pigeon lady the vowels she needs, then she'll be able to—um—communicate with people, and the problem will be over."

Rachel waited.

"That's my idea."

"Give vowels to the pigeon lady."

"Yep."

"Vowels made out of?"

"Well, I have some cardboard," said Brian.

"I have some sheets of Styrofoam," Rachel said. "Different colors. That would be better."

"Neat," breathed Brian.

Now Rachel considered. Large letters made out of colored Styrofoam. Vowels. Delivered as a gift to the pigeon lady. If she would let them in—two innocent little kids bringing her a gift, why wouldn't she?—Rachel might have a chance to look around her house, to find out—what?

Well, who knew what she'd be able to find out? Anything might be useful, might help Uncle Benson to come up with another plan and help the pigeon lady before the neighbors sold her house out from under her and sent her off to an old folks' home whether she wanted to live in one or not.

"Vowels!" Rachel said. "Brian, that's a great idea!"

"I know," Brian said, blushing with happiness.

"But let's keep it a secret, okay? Just between the two of us."

Brian shook his head yes. He loved secrets!

"I'll bring the Styrofoam and some scissors and templates for letters over to your house tomorrow morning. We can make the letters and then take them over to the pigeon lady's house in the afternoon. If we're lucky, she'll let us in and we can, um, explain the letters to her and tell her what they sound like and how to use them in words and stuff. Okay?"

"Okay, Rachel, but not too early in the morning. I'm having breakfast with my dad tomorrow. Sunday morning. You know." Brian's parents were divorced. He had breakfast with his dad on Sunday mornings. "I'll be home by noon."

"Okay, I'll see you at noon," Rachel said. "If we don't finish in time, we'll take them over Monday after school. And remember, it's a secret."

"I'll remember, Rachel," Brian said. "And you remember, it was *my* idea!"

"Don't worry, Brian," Rachel said, "that's something I definitely won't forget!"

Happy and satisfied, off he went.

Rachel started upstairs to get the supplies they'd need. She felt a little scared, thinking about going into the pigeon lady's creepy, falling-down house, with just Brian.

"Nothing to be scared of," she told herself firmly. "One weird old lady. What could there possibly be to be scared of?"

Still, she thought.

Don't be ridiculous, Rachel, she thought.

Well, she thought.

Enough of this! she decided as she walked down the hall to her bedroom.

She could hear Lesley's voice on the telephone, talking to Luz.

Rachel closed her door, so she wouldn't have to hear. Then she lay down on her bed and looked out her window at the sky. She looked at the pieces of it she could see between the large, dark green leaves of the avocado tree, one that Jonathan and her father had started from an ordinary pit they got out of an avocado and sprouted in some water and then planted in the ground.

They said they never really expected it to grow at all, let alone grow into a tree, way up to the roof of the house. And here it was, tall and vigorous, practically blocking all the light that should have come into Rachel's room through her bedroom window.

Rachel didn't mind. She loved the avocado tree's

dark green leaves. She loved how proud Jonathan was of the surprising plant. She loved its unusual history. She much preferred viewing the sky in bits and pieces through the leaves of an avocado tree than any other way.

6

Rachel and Brian finished making the letters too late on Sunday to take them to the pigeon lady's. They made a plan to go right after school on Monday.

Rachel had spent all of Sunday afternoon with Brian at his kitchen table, working on the vowels. It turned out to be a lot of work, and harder than she thought it would be. Brian's mom, who was good at art projects, had ended up helping them. When she asked them why they were making Styrofoam vowels, Rachel fibbed and told her it was an exercise for Brian, to help him remember his vowels. And Brian pressed his lips tightly together and looked at his mother with his eyes so wide that Rachel was sure Mrs. Bishop would know that she was lying.

But Mrs. Bishop was so interested in making the letters that she didn't notice. And besides, she thought it was a great idea to teach in such an entertaining way.

"Uncle Benson is so clever," she told Rachel, "figuring out different ways to teach people, using all their senses. Why, Brian is never going to forget his vowels now that he's cut them out and handled them—are you, Brian?"

"Nope, never!" declared Brian. "*A, E, I, O, U, Y,*" he recited loudly.

"And it's kind of you to help, Rachel," Mrs. Bishop said.

"I like to," Rachel said. "And Uncle Benson is really busy. He can't do everything himself."

Then she remembered to stop talking. Lesley and Jonathan had taught her a long time ago, when you're telling a lie, keep it *simple.*

"Of course he can't," said Mrs. Bishop. "Well, he doesn't have to do everything himself. All he has to do is think of things. Other people can put his ideas into play. Right, Brian?"

Brian was carefully trimming a large red letter *A.* "Mmm," he agreed, not looking at his mother.

Rachel ate dinner at the Bishops', and when she got home, who was standing at her own front door but Uncle Benson and Mr. Gioia! Uncle Benson saw her. "Hi, Rach," he called. She came forward slowly and waited at the bottom of the steps while the men finished talking.

"You'll think about what I've said, won't you, Greg?" asked Uncle Benson.

"Yes, yes," said Mr. Gioia, not sounding very sincere. Then he hurried down the steps right past Rachel and on down the street.

"What was that about, Uncle Benson?" Rachel asked as they went into the house.

"I'm not really sure," he answered. "I invited Mr. Gioia over to chat about the pigeon lady and about his plan. I hoped we could come up with something a little better, from Mrs. Krnc's point of view . . ."

"Did you?"

Uncle Benson shook his head. "No, we didn't. I made a couple of suggestions. But nothing I thought of interested Mr. Gioia." Uncle Benson sighed. Then he changed the subject. "So what were you and Brian up to all afternoon?" he asked.

"Common sense and fowls," Rachel said. "I was helping Brian. He really wants to learn all the stuff you're teaching him. He, um, he doesn't want to disappoint you. Actually, he wants to amaze you with how quickly he can learn when he puts his mind to it. So I was helping him get started. He knows all his 'fowls' now."

"We'll review vowels first thing when I meet with him, then, so he can amaze me," said Uncle Benson, chuckling.

"What about the pigeon lady, Uncle Benson? What are we going to do?"

"I don't know, Rachel. This is a tough one." Uncle Benson stared into space. Then he smiled. "Maybe I'll just do whatever Lesley and her friends are thinking of doing. Carry a sign. Shout slogans. E-mail the governor. Hold a silent vigil."

"Are they going to do all those things?"

"That's just the short list!" said Uncle Benson. "They've been studying lawful democratic protest in their American history class. I think they want to make the neighborhood into a laboratory where they can try out all the things they've been reading about."

Rachel knew Uncle Benson was unhappy about his meeting with Mr. Gioia. And she could tell he was still stumped.

She had her work cut out for her!

After school Monday, Rachel and Brian came home for a quick snack, wrapped the letters in a colorful old beach towel Rachel found in the basement, and set off for Mrs. Krnc's.

"What if she's outside feeding the pigeons?" Brian wanted to know.

"We'll wait up by Mr. Twiddle's until she goes back inside," Rachel said.

"What if there's a bunch of neighbors outside her house?" he asked.

"We'll have to wait until they leave," Rachel said.

"What if that old man is back?"

"Then we'll have to wait until *he* leaves."

Luckily, the coast was clear.

Nobody was around, and even though a few pigeons still pecked about at the remains of a feeding, the pigeon lady herself was nowhere to be seen.

But at the last minute, Brian hung back. "I'm scared, Rachel. She might be mean. She looks mean. She looks like a mean old *witch*!"

"Stop that, Brian!" Rachel said firmly. "And come on. We've got to get inside before somebody comes along. Mrs. Krnc'll never let us in if there's someone else out here."

Rachel carried the big letters under one arm, and with her other hand she dragged Brian up the front walk, up the sagging steps, and onto the porch.

"Ring the bell," Rachel whispered.

Brian stuck out one finger and poked at the door-

bell as if it might bite him. "I didn't hear it ring," he said.

"Me neither. I bet it's broken."

They waited. Nothing happened.

Rachel let go of Brian's hand. She was relieved when he just stood by her side. She'd been afraid he might take off if she wasn't hanging on to him. She knocked loudly. Nothing. She knocked again.

Then she saw the gray rag of a curtain that covered one of the front windows rise and fall and caught a glimpse of Mrs. Krnc as she looked out. She really did look like a witch in a book of fairy tales.

A shiver ran up Rachel's back.

"Rachel, I have to go to the bathroom," Brian said.

"Brian," Rachel whispered, "you do not. You just went."

She knocked again. "Mrs. Krnc," she called, "it's me, Rachel Harris, and my friend Brian Bishop. We've brought something for you. We made you a present. Can we come in?"

"Rachel, she doesn't speak English," Brian reminded her.

"I know that, Brian," said Rachel. "But they said she understands some, remember?"

They waited for what seemed to be a long time.

Just as Rachel was about to knock and call out again, they heard sounds behind the door, shuffly sounds, like shuffly footsteps on bare floors, and then the creaky old door slowly opened, and the pigeon lady peered out.

With her free hand, Rachel quickly pulled Brian around so he was standing in front of her. "Look up and *smile*," she whispered, squeezing his shoulder.

Brian threw back his head and smiled a terrified smile, all teeth and staring eyes. Rachel fake-smiled, too.

"Hello, Mrs. Krnc," she said.

"Hi, Mrs. Krnc," said Brian through his closed teeth.

Mrs. Krnc looked curiously down at Brian, as if he were some new sort of creature she'd never seen before. Then she looked back at Rachel.

"We've brought you a present, Mrs. Krnc," Rachel said again. Boldly, she put one foot into the house. "May we come in?"

Mrs. Krnc backed up, and Rachel and Brian followed her into her musty-smelling living room, which was full of sagging chairs and sofas and of small tables crowded with faded photographs.

Once they were inside, Mrs. Krnc stood gazing at the children and looking worried.

Rachel pretended to feel confident. "I guess we'll just sit down, if that's all right," she said in a friendly voice.

She pushed Brian ahead of her, and they both sat down on a small sofa.

Mrs. Krnc looked less worried once Rachel and Brian were sitting down, and she sat, too. She clasped her hands between her knees, stared at them, and smiled.

Rachel smiled back. So did Brian. The three of them sat for a couple of minutes, smiling. Without taking his eyes off the pigeon lady or changing his expression, Brian said, "Rachel, aren't you going to give her the vowels?'

And without taking *her* eyes off the pigeon lady or changing *her* expression, Rachel answered, "Of course I am, Brian."

Mrs. Krnc looked from one of them to the other, the worried expression now back on her face.

"Mrs. Krnc," Rachel said loudly, "we've made you something we know you can use!" Mrs. Krnc gave Rachel her attention. Rachel stood up, and took the towel off the Styrofoam letters. "Ta—da!" she announced.

Mrs. Krnc looked interested.

"Vowels!" said Rachel. She held the letters up, one by one. "*A, E, I, O, U, Y!*" she said.

"Vowels, Mrs. Krnc," said Brian, standing up, too, and hopping excitedly from one foot to the other, "so you can—um—communicate better with your neighbors and solve your problems. So they won't sell your house and send you away!"

"Brian!"

"I mean, so you can speak English, Mrs. Krnc," Brian said.

Smiling, Mrs. Krnc gently touched the letters, one by one. It was clear she liked the gift. She held up a finger as if to say, wait here, and disappeared through a doorway that led into another part of the house. Then she was back, lugging an old wooden ladder.

She set the ladder up against the wall, and with the letters under her arm, she clambered up.

While Rachel and Brian watched, she carefully arranged the vowels along the old-fashioned molding that ran around the top of the room, a couple of feet below the ceiling. The letters were backwards and upside down and in no particular order, and she arranged and rearranged them, climbing up and down many times, until she was satisfied with the way they looked.

When she finished, she stood back to admire her work.

"Ahhh," she said, smiling, and then something that sounded to Rachel and Brian like "Zmnftch!"

"She thinks they're just for decoration," said Brian.

"I know," said Rachel.

"But they do look nice," he added loyally.

Rachel had to agree. "They do," she said.

Mrs. Krnc waved her arm, gesturing so the children would take in the full effect of the colorful letters.

While Mrs. Krnc was busy arranging the vowels, Rachel had looked carefully around the room, at the old photographs and odds and ends of stuff. She'd realized there was no way she was going to be able to find out anything that would be of use to Uncle Benson just by poking around Mrs. Krnc's house. She'd have to think of something else.

"We should get going now, Brian," Rachel said. They stood up to leave.

But the pigeon lady had another idea.

7

Mrs. Krnc motioned for Rachel and Brian to stay, the way you might motion to a dog—"Stay!"—and backed out of the room, keeping her eyes right on them. Neither of them dared move.

They heard noises in the next room.

"What do you think she's doing now?" Brian asked.

Just then the old woman popped back in. Brian felt the way he felt when he was caught talking in class and he shouldn't be.

She was gesturing, trying to say something to them. She was pantomiming. What? Drinking, eating.

"She's saying she's making us something to eat," Rachel guessed.

"Great!" said Brian.

Mrs. Krnc disappeared again.

Now Rachel and Brian could hear quite a commotion coming from what must be the kitchen. As long as they were staying, Rachel decided she would take a more careful look around.

She started with some of the old black-and-white photographs crowded onto a small table by the side of a shabby easy chair.

"Look at this," she said, holding one up for Brian to see.

Brian was becoming alarmed. "Put that down, Rachel. She'll catch you."

"I'll hear when she stops banging. Come look."

Brian and Rachel studied the pictures.

Here was a young woman in a cross-stitched peasant blouse with a thick braid of dark hair wound around the top of her head, staring into the camera.

Here was the same young woman standing next to a handsome young man a head shorter than she was. He was dressed all in white and had one arm around her waist.

And here were two rows of middle-aged men and women who looked as if having their picture taken was something that made them very uncomfortable. They were dressed in some sort of costumes. If they had been younger and had looked happier, they might have been dancers posing for a publicity shot.

"She's coming!" Brian warned.

Hastily, Rachel replaced the picture. She and Brian sat back down.

The pigeon lady came in carrying a big tray loaded with a platter of lumpy cookies, a teapot with a faded flowery pattern, and chipped china cups and saucers. So many different spicy smells came in with her, Rachel and Brian had no idea what she might be bringing them to eat or drink.

"Poison," Brian muttered.

"Don't be silly," said Rachel, not sounding so sure.

Mrs. Krnc balanced the large tray on a teetery table in front of the sofa. Then she pulled up a teetery chair to sit on.

She poured three cups of what turned out to be watery ginger tea. And she passed around the plate of spice cookies. The cookies were so hard, Rachel was sure she would chip a tooth if she tried to bite into one. Manners or no manners, she decided, she was going to dunk hers. Brian followed her lead. The pigeon lady was already dunking away. But she had no choice. She had no teeth.

There they sat eating spice cookies dunked in ginger tea and listening as the pigeon lady told them a long, sad-sounding tale they could not understand. But because of the emotion in her voice and the tears in her eyes, Rachel knew that the pigeon lady was telling them, in between swigs of awful tea and swallows of soggy cookie, things that mattered to her, important things about herself. It didn't seem fair for them to sit there and pretend to be understanding her. But what else could they do?

Finally Rachel put her hand on the pigeon lady's wrist. "Wait, Mrs. Krnc, wait a minute, please," she said.

The pigeon lady pulled her hand away.

"Mrs. Krnc," Rachel said, "please don't be afraid. I just wanted to tell you, we can't understand what you're trying to say to us. And we'd like to. That's why we came today. To find out. To understand. To get to know you so we can figure out some way to help. We want to be your friends, Mrs. Krnc. But we don't understand your language. We don't know what you're trying to tell us."

Mrs. Krnc got up and went to sit in the saggy easy chair. Her face now wore an unhappy expression.

"We should leave, Rachel," Brian said. "This wasn't a good idea."

"She liked the vowels," Rachel reminded him,

pointing at the colorful letters marching around the ceiling.

Mrs. Krnc looked up at the letters. She smiled and nodded.

"I still think it's time for us to go," said Brian.

Rachel was about ready to agree when she remembered the photographs. "One more try, Brian," she said.

She got up and went to stand next to the pigeon lady.

"We were wondering, Mrs. Krnc," she said, "who is this?"

Rachel held up the picture of the girl with the braid. A pleased look pulled at the corners of the pigeon lady's mouth. She kept her hands in her lap, but with the slightest flicker of one finger she pointed to herself.

"You!" Rachel said happily. "This must be a picture of you when you were young, when you were in your own country!"

Rachel put down that picture and picked up the one of the same girl and the young man dressed in white. "And what about this one, Mrs. Krnc?" she asked. "Who is this?"

The old woman took the picture and held it to her heart, smiling. Then, shyly, she handed it back to Rachel.

"This must be a picture of your husband!" Rachel said.

Nothing would satisfy Mrs. Krnc after that but to try to tell Rachel and Brian her story—at least the part of it involving the love of her life, her dead husband, Mr. Krnc.

Mrs. Krnc, with her skinny arms and legs, her lopsided kerchief and matted hair, her toothless grin, her faded sweater, her droopy dungarees, was remarkably good at acting things out. Now she was an innocent country girl living with her strict parents in a mountain village. Now she was surprised to be courted by a lively, handsome visitor from the big city. Now her heart was won by his most inventive ploy: he surprised her by walking all about on his hands before he asked her to marry him.

Mrs. Krnc, at that point in her wordless story, amazed the children by doing the same thing! With her spidery legs in the air and her baggy slacks bunching around her knees, the old lady walked on her hands around the room.

But she didn't end up gracefully on one knee in a position to propose marriage, as the young Mr. Krnc probably did. She toppled over, red in the face, with her matted brown hair and faded kerchief lying on the floor nearby!

"Mrs. Krnc," Rachel cried, "are you all right?"

No answer.

"Brian, help me get her up!"

Together, Rachel and Brian got the old woman to the sofa and helped her stretch out. As her eyes became less cloudy, the first thing she did was touch the top of her head and then try to get up.

"Her hair!" Rachel guessed. "Brian, get her hair!"

Brian got the sad-looking wig with the kerchief attached, and shyly handed it to Mrs. Krnc. She slid it onto her head and sank back down.

Then she reached out toward the table with the pictures on it. Rachel brought her the picture of herself with her husband. She hugged it to her. She reached out again. Rachel brought her the picture of herself as a young woman. She hugged that picture to her. She reached out again. Rachel brought her the picture of the middle-aged people in their costumes. She hugged that tight and reached out again. Over and over, Rachel brought the pigeon lady a picture. Over and over, the woman hugged the picture and reached out for another. Soon her arms were full of pictures.

"Hm," the pigeon lady said. "Hm."

"Hm?" Rachel wondered.

"She means *home*," Brian said.

"She does?" said Rachel. "How do you know?"

"I can tell," said Brian. "She doesn't have any vowels. *Hm* is just *home* without vowels."

"Brian," Rachel said, "that's brilliant!"

"I know," said Brian.

"Mrs. Krnc," Rachel said, "is it home? Do you want to go home?"

The old lady, who had been so animated walking on her hands just a few minutes before, now turned toward Rachel the saddest face Rachel had ever seen. She nodded. "Hm," she said.

"But, Mrs. Krnc, why don't you just go, then?" Rachel asked.

Mrs. Krnc slowly pushed aside her sorry-looking wig and pointed to her bald head.

"You don't have a nice wig," Rachel guessed.

Mrs. Krnc nodded yes.

Mrs. Krnc pointed to her mouth.

"You don't have any teeth," said Rachel softly.

Mrs. Krnc nodded yes.

Then Mrs. Krnc rubbed her thumb and fingers together in the universal sign that people use to mean money, and she shrugged and looked forlorn.

"And you don't have enough money?"

Mrs. Krnc nodded yes.

"Mrs. Krnc," Rachel said kindly, "now that I

know what you want and what you need, I know how people can help you. And I think everything is going to be all right. But you have to help, too. You have to do your part. You have to stop feeding the pigeons." Rachel pantomimed pigeon-feeding and, frowning, very emphatically shook her head no. "Can you do that?"

Mrs. Krnc looked worried.

"Will you try?"

The old lady stood up. She didn't shake her head to say yes. But she didn't shake it to say no, either.

"We have to go now, Mrs. Krnc. But we'll be back," Rachel told her as she and Brian headed for the door.

Mrs. Krnc followed them. Catching hold of Brian, she stuffed some of the awful ginger cookies into his pockets. Then she patted him on the head and, with her arm around his shoulder, shuffled along with him and Rachel to the door.

When Rachel and Brian were halfway down the walk, they looked back. The door was closed. There was no sign of anyone moving around behind the curtains.

"If I didn't have these cookies in my pocket, I'd think we dreamed all of that, Rachel," Brian said.

8

Before Brian went home, he dug the cookies out of his pocket. "Here, Rach," he said, "you better take these."

"Right," Rachel agreed. They didn't want Brian's mom asking questions. Rachel shoved them in her pocket. "I'll throw them away later," she said, "destroy the evidence."

Brian liked that. "Destroy the evidence," he repeated, smiling. "Okay, bye, Rachel."

"Bye, Brian." She turned to go.

"Rachel?"

"Brian?"

"I have another idea."

"Another idea about what?"

"About how to help the pigeon lady."

"Do you think it can wait until tomorrow, Brian?

I'm kind of tired of the pigeon lady right now. And I have homework to do."

"And you have evidence to destroy."

"That, too. So can it wait?"

"I guess," he said. "But can I tell you tomorrow?"

"Sure. Tomorrow."

"When tomorrow, Rachel?"

Rachel sighed. "After school tomorrow, Brian."

"Uncle Benson's going to tutor me after school tomorrow."

"After that, then."

"Okay," he said. "But don't forget. You won't forget, will you?"

Rachel gave Brian a long look. "I. Won't. Forget," she said.

Brian smiled. "Okay," he said. "It's a really good idea, Rachel. And it's a secret, too!"

"I won't tell anybody," Rachel promised.

Rachel found Lesley and her friends Luz and Dewayna at the dining room table, busily working.

"What's up?" she asked.

"We're writing a petition in support of the pigeon lady," Lesley said.

"We're going to collect signatures all around the neighborhood," explained Dewayna.

"We're going to get people to sign who are on the pigeon lady's side," said Luz, "and then we're going to take the signed petition to that judge."

"What judge?"

"To the judge Mr. Gioia said he was going to—the judge who's supposed to get the pigeon lady turned over to a caretaker who'll sell her house. *That* judge, after we find out who it is," said Lesley. "When the judge sees that there are all these people who are on the pigeon lady's side, Mr. Gioia's plan will never work."

"All what people?"

"All the people who sign the petition," said Luz.

"After we get it worded correctly," Dewayna added, "and circulated."

"So don't interrupt us," Lesley said. "We have a lot more work to do!"

In the kitchen, Rachel found Uncle Benson stir-frying vegetables in a wok. He'd already prepared some brown rice. Rachel said hello and got out plates and napkins and forks and chopsticks, too. She filled some glasses with water and opened a bottle of soy sauce.

After the two of them sat down to eat, she asked him about the petition they could hear the girls arguing over in the next room.

"Do you think it'll do any good, Uncle Benson?"

"Well, a petition is a good idea," he said. "But I doubt they'll get many people to sign it. The fact is, what Mrs. Krnc is doing is illegal. And the action Mr. Gioia and the others have decided to take isn't."

Rachel considered this while she ate. "Uncle Benson," she said finally, "what the neighbors are doing seems wrong. If it's legal, why does it seem wrong?"

"I didn't say I thought it was the best possible solution, Rachel. All I said was it's legal."

"Can it be legal and wrong?"

"It can be legal and far less than perfect. I think with some extra time and effort, we'd all be able to come up with something better. But Mr. Gioia and the Elm Avenue neighbors are in a hurry."

"This is too complicated, Uncle Benson," Rachel said.

"It is complicated," he agreed, helping himself to more rice and the last of the vegetables.

Rachel pushed her plate away. She took one of the spice cookies out of her pocket and tapped it on the top of the table.

"Careful," said Uncle Benson. "You might scratch the tabletop with that rock."

"It's not a rock, Uncle Benson," Rachel said, "it's a cookie." She held it up for him to see.

"A cookie? I've never seen a cookie hard enough to bang on a table and not leave a single crumb. What kind of cookie is it?"

Rachel squinted playfully at him. "Oh, just a plain old spice cookie, Uncle Benson," she said. She shoved it across. Then she took the others out of her pocket and shoved them over, too.

He eyed them doubtfully. "Cookies? Are you sure?"

"Mmm-hmmm. Brian and I got them when we had tea over at Mrs. Krnc's this afternoon."

"*Tea* at Mrs. Krnc's?"

"Me and Brian."

"Rachel! How did you get her to let you in?"

Rachel leaned across the table. "We took her some vowels!" she confided.

"Vowels?"

"She already has plenty of consonants, Uncle Benson."

"Rachel, what on earth are you talking about?"

"When we were at the meeting on Saturday, somebody said if the pigeon lady had vowels, she'd be able to communicate with people. Remember? And Brian got the idea of making vowels for her. To help her communicate and to solve the problem."

"But Rachel, you knew . . . I mean, you did know that Brian's idea was generous, but that it couldn't . . ."

"Couldn't work? Of course I knew," Rachel said. "But I figured if I could just get into her house, maybe I could find out something that would help *you* figure out how to help her."

"And?" Uncle Benson asked eagerly.

Rachel made a disappointed face.

"Didn't work out that way?"

"Wellll," she said slowly, "we did find out *some* things . . ."

"Like?"

"Like, she makes the worst cookies and the barfiest tea in the world."

"Oh."

"And . . ."

"Yes?"

"And the inside of her house is a mess."

"Oh."

"And . . ."

"Yes?"

"And Mrs. Krnc is completely bald. That hair underneath her scarf is fake. They're attached. They both come off together."

"Really? Why'd she take them off?"

"She didn't. They fell off when she walked on her hands."

"Walked on her hands?"

"To show us how her husband walked around on *his* hands when he asked her to marry him."

"Her husband?"

"A long, long time ago!"

"I bet it was!" Uncle Benson smiled. "Why, Rachel, you managed to find out an awful lot about Mrs. Krnc. How in the world did you do it?"

"But wait, Uncle Benson, that's not all," Rachel said. "Here's the most important part of what we found out: Mrs. Krnc is not happy. What she really wants most of all is hm."

"Hm?"

"Hm. She wants to go there."

"Hmmm," mused Uncle Benson. "Hm. Hm? Oh! Home! She wants to go *home*!" he said. "I get it!"

"But she can't," said Rachel. She waited.

"I'm listening," he said. "Go on. She can't because . . ."

"Because she doesn't have a good wig. And she doesn't have any teeth. And she doesn't have enough money."

"Rachel, how did she tell you all this?"

"She's great at pantomime, Uncle Benson," Rachel

explained. "We should ask her over whenever we play charades. She's really a genius at acting things out."

"You're a genius at *finding* things out."

"And Brian. Don't forget Brian. The vowels were his idea. They're what got us in."

"Yes, yes, and Brian. Brian is a genius, too." Uncle Benson was thoughtful. "The question is, how can we use the information now?"

"What do you mean, 'now'?"

"I mean now that her neighbors have their plan under way. It's so hard to get people to change once they've got their minds made up."

"Even if we have a better, more just plan?" asked Rachel.

Uncle Benson didn't answer.

"We do have a better, more just plan, don't we, Uncle Benson?"

"Actually, we don't, Rachel, not yet. But we will. Soon. Let's have dessert and see if we can think of one."

"Uncle Benson, I have a ton of homework to do," Rachel reminded him. "And I'm stuffed."

"Then I'll get busy and try to think of one," he replied. "Over a dish of something sweet . . ."

Rachel went upstairs feeling completely satisfied.

She and Brian had done what they'd set out to do. The satisfaction she felt was every bit as sweet as dessert.

After Rachel finished her homework, she came back downstairs, ready to hear all about Uncle Benson's plan. But he wasn't busy polishing up the details of a new plan that would meet the needs of the neighbors and the pigeon lady, too. He was fast asleep on the couch.

Rachel tiptoed into the living room to turn off the light.

As soon as she did, he woke up.

"Rachel?" he said, "Is that you? What time is it?"

"Time for bed, Uncle Benson," she said.

"My, I'm tired," he mumbled. "I need a different means of transportation. I need a different way of doing business. This is just not working anymore. I'm too old to be a roving tutor. I need a home base now."

"Uncle Benson, are you awake?"

"What's that? I think I am. Yes, I am. Why?"

"I just wondered. Have you thought of a plan?"

"I have. I've thought of a plan."

"Great! What is it?"

"I'm going to find a place where I can have my students come to me instead of me going to them."

"What?"

"That's my plan."

"How will that help?"

"I'll be able to see more students, and I'll save energy for teaching."

"I mean, how will it help the pigeon lady? How will it help the neighbors?"

"It won't. It will help me. It'll help my students."

"Uncle Benson, you said you'd think of a plan."

"And I have!"

"But you've thought of the wrong plan!"

"What's wrong with it?"

"It doesn't help the right people is what's wrong with it!"

Silence.

Uncle Benson shook his head. Now he was fully awake.

"Rachel," he said, "exactly what is it you and I are talking about?"

9

After Uncle Benson finished tutoring
Brian, he went on to another student. But he left his
bicycle in the garage and drove Mr. Twiddle's delivery
truck. His plan to have a place where his students
could come to him, he'd realized, would have to wait.
"That's the pie-in-the-sky plan," he told Rachel.
"Something to dream about." For now, he would
have to solve his problem more quickly. He would
have to replace the bike with some kind of vehicle.
"Maybe a van like this one," he told Rachel, who
was going into the Bishops' as he was coming out. "I
could deliver education from place to place the way
Mr. Twiddle delivers groceries. This week, I'll be delivering both!"

"Both?" asked Rachel.

"I'm borrowing Mr. Twiddle's van until I figure
out exactly what I need to get for myself. And until I

find time to shop for it. In return for the use of the van, I'm handling the grocery deliveries, too. Luckily, most people want groceries delivered in the morning, and most people want tutoring in the afternoons and evenings, so delivering both should work out pretty well. At least for a while."

"How many deliveries today?"

"Education or food?"

"Food."

"Just one, actually. Mr. Damesek."

"The painter?"

"The painter."

"That's interesting."

Uncle Benson waited. But when it became clear that Rachel wasn't going to tell him why she thought it was interesting, he went on his way. And so did she.

Brian was at his front door, jiggling with excitement.

"So what's up, Brian?" Rachel asked.

"Shhh," he reminded her, putting his finger to his lips.

"So what's up, Brian?" Rachel whispered.

Brian motioned for Rachel to follow him to his room.

"What a mess!" she exclaimed as they stepped inside and he closed the door.

"Be careful not to step on anything that could break," he warned, leaping onto his unmade bed.

Rachel took off her shoes and gingerly made her way over to the bed. She knew how upset Brian would be if she accidentally stepped on one of his treasures. But it was tricky, since there was no way of telling where one might be.

"What's up?" she asked again, when she finally made it to the bed and flopped down on her back, studying the stars and planets he'd had his mom paste on his ceiling. "What's your idea?"

"Guess!"

"Brian, I'm not going to guess."

"Oh, come on, Rachel."

She started to get up again.

"Okay, okay," he said, grabbing for the back of her shirt. "Sit down, Rachel."

"I'll stand. Now tell me."

"Rachel!"

"Oh, okay." She sat back down. "Now tell me, Brian."

"*Consonants,*" he whispered.

"Consonants?"

"Consonants."

"What about them?"

"Well, remember we took vowels to Mrs. Krnc?"

"Of course I remember. We just did it yesterday. Remember?"

"Of course I remember."

"So?"

"So now we need to make consonants. To take to Mr. Gioia!" Brian was so happy with his idea that he started to giggle and had to clamp both hands over his mouth and then bury his face in his smashed-up pillow.

Rachel waited until he got control of himself and could sit up again. Then she said. "Why?"

"Why what?"

"Why take consonants to Mr. Gioia?"

"Because he needs them."

"What makes you think so?"

"Look at his name, Rach. He has one teensy little consonant in his whole name. The pigeon lady needed vowels. And he needs consonants. We made friends with Mrs. Krnc when we brought her vowels. And if we take consonants to Mr. Gioia, we'll make friends with him. And then we'll be friends with both of them, and—"

"Brian . . ."

"Yes?"

"Stop."

"Why?"

"It's not a good idea."

"It is too!"

"No it's not."

"Yes it is!"

"Not."

"Is!"

"Not!"

Brian stood up on the bed. "Why not?"

"Because Mr. Gioia doesn't have *any* trouble communicating! He communicates all over the place. He communicates with everybody. He speaks English perfectly. He doesn't need any consonants. It's different!"

"But he only has one dinky little consonant in his whole last name, Rachel. And I bet if we made him big Styrofoam consonants in different colors and took them over to his house he'd let us in and we'd find stuff out about him just like we did about the pigeon lady. And then."

"What, and then?"

"Something. And then something," Brian said.

"It's a dumb idea, Brian. Forget it."

"I'm not going to forget it, Rachel," he said. "You forget it."

"I will," she said. "I have. I've already forgotten it. I've forgotten it, and I'm leaving now. I'm going home."

"Fine. And I'm doing it anyway."

"You're what?"

"I'm doing it anyway."

"How are you?"

"My mom will help me. I'll tell her I need to do the same project, except with consonants, for Uncle Benson."

"And then what?"

"And then I'll take them to Mr. Gioia's house, and I'll give them to him."

"Fine."

"You're supposed to say, 'Brian, I can't let you go there by yourself.' "

Silence.

"Rachel?"

Silence.

"Rachel, you can't let me go there by myself!"

"I know I can't, Brian."

"And I'm going, Rachel."

"I know you are, Brian."

"So—you're coming with me, right, Rachel?"

Silence.

"Right, Rachel?"

Sigh. "Right, Brian."

Rachel and Brian started on the consonants that afternoon. Rachel decided they didn't have time to do all of them. "Six vowels, six consonants," Rachel said. "Even steven."

"Even steven," Brian said and laughed. He liked that. "Which ones should we do?" he asked.

"Just pick the ones you like, Brian," Rachel said.

Brian had a hard time making up his mind. Finally he chose *B*, for Brian and Benson, *R* for Rachel, *M* for Mom, *K* for Krnc, *P* for pigeons, and *G* for Gioia. "Just one more?" he begged.

"Which one?"

"*L*, for luck."

Rachel gave in. "Okay."

"More letters, that's great," said Brian's mother.

"Consonants," said Rachel.

"Uncle Benson is lucky to have you," Mrs. Bishop told her again. "Especially when he's so tired."

"He has the van now," Rachel said. "Mr. Twiddle's grocery van. He's probably going to get one of his own. When he has time."

"That'll make things easier. Still, he's going to have to figure out a better way to work. He's going to have to set himself up someplace so students can come to him. Even driving around in a van, he's got too many places to go every day."

"Especially since he's delivering groceries for Mr. Twiddle, too," Rachel said, not looking up from the blue *L* she was starting to cut out.

"Delivering groceries, too!" Mrs. Bishop said. "I didn't know that. I think I'll call and place a grocery order for next time he comes here!"

Mr. Gioia wasn't home all the time, the way the pigeon lady was. He was hardly ever home. Rachel and Brian had to check after school to see whether his car was wrapped up and parked in the ten-minute zone in front of Twiddle's Fine Foods. If it was, they knew Mr. Gioia would probably be at his house.

The consonants were ready by Friday. After school, Rachel and Brian put them into a large plastic Christmas bag Rachel had saved. Then they hurried up the hill to Twiddle's. Sure enough, Mr. Gioia's car was parked right where it shouldn't be. By now everyone was used to having it there. Nobody expected to find a ten-minute parking space right in front of the store anymore. They knew that until the pigeon prob-

91

lem was settled, Mr. Gioia's car would usually be parked there.

Now, as Rachel and Brian came up the hill toward the store, there it was, all wrapped up. But as they got closer, they saw there was something different about the wrapping.

"What's that, Rachel?" Brian wanted to know.

"What's what?"

"There's something on the back of Mr. Gioia's car. Something painted on the tarp he's got covering his car. Is it a bird?"

"It does look like a bird," Rachel said, walking faster.

"Wait up, Rachel."

"Hurry up, Brian."

It was a bird. It was the same kind of bird that was painted on the wall at the library! Except this one wasn't painted on. It was spray-painted. It was a graffiti bird.

"It's beautiful!" Brian said.

It *was* beautiful. It was a big fantastical flying bird, spray-painted by a talented artist. By the same artist who'd painted the birds on the wall at the library. Mr. Damesek!

Rachel could not picture the ancient man in the long black coat sneaking around the neighborhood with cans of spray paint. It was beyond imagining. But she was sure nobody else could have created this bird.

"I hope Mr. Gioia hasn't seen this yet," she said.

"Why, Rach? Don't you think he'll like it? It's pretty!"

"I *don't* think he'll like it, Brian. I don't think he'll like somebody graffitiing his car."

"Not his *car*, Rachel. Just the wrapping."

"Anything of his!"

"How do you spell *graffitiing*?" Brian wanted to know.

Rachel wasn't sure. "Why?" she said.

"I was just wondering," he said, "about vowels. And consonants." He giggled. "It's a funny word."

"It's a funny word, but that's about all that's funny about it. What was Mr. Damesek thinking?"

"That he was helping the pigeon lady?"

"I guess."

"Or maybe he just wanted to show off what a good artist he is," said Brian.

"Maybe. Anyway, let's go to Mr. Gioia's, Brian, and get this over with before things get even more complicated."

"Should we tell him about the graffiti?"

Rachel could see that Brian was excited. She made herself sound very calm. "Oh, no," she said. "I don't think we need to mention it, Brian. Why spoil the— um—surprise? Let's just stick to our—your—plan. Let's just stick with consonants, and communication, and solving the neighborhood problem. Let's not talk about graffiti. Not today. It might just get too . . ."

"Too exciting!" said Brian.

"Right," Rachel agreed. "Just. Too. Exciting."

Brian fairly danced down the hill and along Elm Avenue to Mr. Gioia's. Rachel plodded. She felt as if her ankles had weights around them. And as they passed the pigeon lady's, she thought she saw a dark-coated figure duck behind the ragged, overgrown bushes at the side of the house.

10

The pigeon lady had been feeding the birds again. Her place and the yards and houses near hers were a mess.

"Uh-oh," said Brian.

"Think we should skip it?" Rachel asked.

Brian stuck out his chin and looked stubborn. "No," he said.

"Just checking."

They marched on.

"Rachel," Brian said, "did you see that bird?"

"What bird?"

"The graffiti bird."

"Where?"

"On Mrs. Krnc's door. Sort of down by the door-knob."

Rachel slowed almost to a stop. "I didn't see it."

"You can check it out on the way back."

"Was it the same, Brian?"

"The same as what?"

"Was it the same as the one on Mr. Gioia's car?"

"Yep. Dark brown and light brown and flying and wild-looking. Really neat."

"Mr. Damesek!"

"I never heard of a hundred-year-old man running around spray-painting graffiti before, did you, Rachel?"

"I don't think he's really a hundred, Brian."

"You know what I mean. He's *old* to be doing stuff like that."

Rachel had to agree. It was puzzling to think of that old, old man sneaking around the neighborhood with cans of spray paint hidden away in the deep pockets of his long, black coat.

"I guess he's making sure everybody knows which side *he's* on, huh, Rachel?" Brian said.

"I guess," she answered. "Well, here we are."

They were in front of Mr. Gioia's. And it was clear he was home. His walk was swept and his steps and wrought-iron railings were scrubbed. The front of his house as well as his roof had been hosed down, and his lawn had been raked. Everything that could be done to clean up after the pigeons' newest assault had already been done. And on the front door there hung a sign that said WET PAINT. The door shone with a fresh coat of black paint.

Rachel and Brian were careful not to touch it.

"Ring the bell, Brian," Rachel said.

Brian stuck out one finger and poked at the doorbell as if it were alive and might bite him, just the way he'd poked at the pigeon lady's bell.

Even though Brian's finger had barely touched the doorbell, they heard loud, musical chimes, followed by sharp swift steps, and Mr. Gioia's voice called out, "Coming!"

In no time flat, the imposing black door with its huge brass knocker swung smoothly open and the tall figure of Mr. Gregory G. Gioia loomed in front of them.

Even though he'd just finished cleaning and painting, Mr. Gioia was spic and span, combed and cleaned, as if he might have just been sitting around doing absolutely nothing but waiting for company.

"Yes?" he said.

Brian looked down at Mr. Gioia's shiny shoes. Rachel poked him, and he remembered to look up and smile. It was the same scared smile he'd turned on Mrs. Krnc, all teeth and staring eyes. Rachel fake-smiled, too. So did Mr. Gioia.

The three of them stood, fake-smiling at one

another for what seemed forever to Rachel and Brian.

"What do you want, children? Collecting money for something?" asked Mr. Gioia.

"No," Rachel said, "nothing like that, Mr. Gioia. We've, um, well, actually, Brian's—this is Brian, I'm Rachel—Brian's made something for you. He's brought you a present. It's his idea. It's part of his schoolwork. It's—can we come in for a minute?"

Mr. Gioia gazed down. Brian was still smiling desperately up at him.

"Well, all right," he said. "Watch the door. Wet paint, as the sign says."

"Did you have to repaint the door because of the pigeons?" Rachel asked.

"Yes," said Mr. Gioia.

"Not graffiti?" Brian said.

Rachel dropped the bag of consonants and slapped both hands over Brian's mouth. Luckily, Mr. Gioia's back was turned. He was leading them into his spotless living room.

"Well, sit down, sit down," he said, "and tell me what you want."

"We came to give you a present, Mr. Gioia," Rachel repeated, after she and Brian were seated next to each other on a spanking-clean sofa.

She handed Brian the Christmas bag, and Brian presented it to Mr. Gioia, who had pulled up a chair across from them.

Mr. Gioia looked into the bag, pulled out the letters, and then looked back at Brian and Rachel.

"Consonants, Mr. Gioia," Brian explained. "We made them. For you. We made vowels for Mrs. Krnc, because a man at the meeting last week said she needed some. And I thought—since you already have so many vowels—in your name, I mean—well, I thought maybe if you had some consonants, you and Mrs. Krnc would be able to—um—communicate—better. And then everybody would get over being mad. And come up with a better plan."

"Brian's studying vowels and consonants," Rachel jumped in to explain. "Brian's a reluctant reader. My Great-Uncle Benson is his tutor . . ."

But Mr. Gioia wasn't listening. He was busy examining the Styrofoam consonants. Clearly, he was pleased.

"These are *very* nice!" he said.

"We didn't make them all," Brian said. "I mean, all the consonants. There's so many! We could make the rest of them some other time." Rachel gave Brian an "Oh, yeah?" look. "Maybe," he added.

"No need, no need," said Mr. Gioia. "These will

do beautifully. See how fine they look, right up here over the fireplace?" He arranged the letters on the mantel, straight up and down and marching along in order. Then he stood back to admire them. "A nice, colorful touch. Don't you agree?" he asked.

Rachel and Brian did agree. The letters looked cheerful in Mr. Gioia's clean, colorless room.

"Now," said Mr. Gioia, "why don't you two come on out into the kitchen? I baked this morning, and I have delicious fresh lemon squares on top of the stove. We can have a snack.

"Before I retired," Mr. Gioia told them over lemon squares and ice-cold milk, "I didn't know a thing about baking. But I've learned. I have so much time on my hands now. And I can't stand not being busy. Retirement," he said, sighing, "can be difficult."

"Really?" asked Brian. "My dad says he can't wait to retire."

"It's all right for some people," Mr. Gioia said. "Might be okay for your dad. But it's not for me. I don't like it at all. I like to keep busy. I like every minute of every day and every night to be filled. And I don't mean busy with leisure activities, golf and what have you. I mean busy with work! Real work."

Rachel thought. "If you want to work, why did you retire?"

"I had to. Rules, you know. The company I worked for had rules. At a certain age, retirement. It was in my contract. I fought it. But—well, here I am, retired. And not happy, I assure you.

"But"—Mr. Gioia swept every crumb off the kitchen table with a clean sponge—"it does give me time to take an interest in everything that's going on around me, neighborhood matters and such. And time to learn to bake, too. How about those lemon squares?"

Brian and Rachel could honestly say they were the best they'd ever tasted. Mr. Gioia looked very pleased. Pleased as punch, as Uncle Benson would have said, mango-pineapple-papaya punch, in fact.

"What else do you do," Brian asked, "to fill up your time?"

"What else?"

"Besides baking?"

"Well, as I said, I take an interest in everything going on around me," Mr. Gioia said. "All the affairs of the neighborhood. Right now, the legal ins and outs of the pigeon problem are taking up a lot of my time. I'm practically becoming a lawyer! And of course I still do the things I've always done as hobbies, carpentry and plumbing and wiring and painting and . . . well, I do whatever needs doing. You might say I'm a *doer*.

"And that reminds me," he went on, "I have quite a few calls to make about this pigeon problem. So many details to take care of . . ." He stood up. "Time for me to get back to business!"

The visit was over. Rachel and Brian were whisked out of the house, politely but firmly. And the shiny black door closed behind them.

Rachel didn't want Brian to think his plan had failed. "Well," she said as they started walking home, "that was interesting, wasn't it."

Brian thought. "The lemon squares were great," he said.

"They were fantastic. And the consonants made Mr. Gioia's living room look a lot better. He needed some color in there."

"Yeah, he needed the consonants," said Brian. "But we didn't find out anything."

"Sure we did, Brian."

"What?"

'Well, we found out that Mr. Gioia's neat and clean and organized."

"We already knew that, Rachel."

"And we found out that he's a great baker."

"Yeah, but that's not going to help."

"You never know," Rachel said.

"It's not, Rachel."

"Well, we found out Mr. Gioia's bored since he retired. That might help Uncle Benson."

"How?"

"I don't know. But it's something nobody understood about Mr. Gioia before. It might be the kind of thing that could help. And it's something we'd never have found out if we hadn't gone over there to give Mr. Gioia consonants. It was a great idea, Brian. I'm glad you thought of it. I'm glad we did it!"

"It was? You are?"

"It was. I am."

Brian grinned goofily and half skipped along next to Rachel. He loved praise.

When they got back, Brian ran to his own house. Rachel turned thoughtfully toward hers.

She could hear her neighbor Mrs. Steiner watering next door, and instead of going inside, she walked down the driveway and around to Mrs. Steiner's side of the tall pyracantha hedge. "Hi, Mrs. Steiner," she said.

Mrs. Steiner kept on watering. "Hello, Rachel," she said. "Want to help?"

"Sure," said Rachel.

"Pull the other hose over, then, and you can spray the flowering beds and the pots. I'll do the herb garden and the vegetables. Some of the seeds have already started to sprout!"

Mrs. Steiner loved her garden. She loved gardens, and she loved books. Mrs. Steiner had been a librarian at the local library branch for years and years, until she retired.

"How do you like being retired, Mrs. Steiner?" Rachel asked as she put on gloves and turned a fine spray onto the newly planted annuals.

"Oh, most of the time I like it," Mrs. Steiner said. "I'm busy as a bee, what with my garden and the Garden Club and writing the monthly garden column for the newspaper. And I'm helping start a gardening program for prisoners at the county jail and another one for the children at my granddaughter's school . . . Sometimes I think I work harder now that I'm retired than I did when I was working!"

Mrs. Steiner pulled on her hose and moved around to the other side of the vegetables.

"But I do miss the library," she said. "I miss being

around all the library smells and the books, and I miss the people, too."

Rachel thought Mrs. Steiner looked sad for a moment.

"Retirement is just different, Rachel," she said briskly. "It's a different time of life. Life has its seasons, you know, just the way gardens do. Spring, summer, fall, winter. Retirement is a different season. You can't compare one season with another, now can you?"

"I guess not," Rachel said.

"Why did you ask?"

"I was just wondering," Rachel said. "I met someone who said he was bored since he retired."

"Oh, that's too bad," said Mrs. Steiner. "There's probably nothing worse than being bored. He needs to find some things to do to keep him busy. Perhaps he needs to take an interest in his community?"

Rachel almost groaned. "Maybe," she said.

"Retired people need to take an interest in something, or they *will* be bored. Well, I'm sure there are books in the library that could help your friend find things that would be of interest to him. You might suggest he try the library."

"Thanks, Mrs. Steiner. I'll do that."

They sprayed the garden in companionable silence for a while.

"You worked at the library for a long time, didn't you, Mrs. Steiner?"

"I did, Rachel." Mrs. Steiner smiled. "I worked there for much longer than I ever thought I would. I came to the library as a very young woman—it was my first job when I got out of college! And I stayed right there for my whole career. I started out as an assistant and ended up as the head librarian. Imagine that! I worked in the same place for more than forty years! I was practically part of the building!"

"Forty years . . . then you must have been there when Mr. Damesek painted the bird wall."

Mrs. Steiner had turned off her hose and was rolling it up. Now she stopped and gazed off into the distance. Her pale eyes seemed to be full of memories. "I was, Rachel," she said. "I most certainly was there when he painted it.

"Actually, I was the only one in the library besides Mr. Damesek that day. The library was closed for painting. I was working back in the children's room, reshelving books. Mr. Damesek was finishing up, painting the last of the walls up in front. He'd been working all week long, painting the walls a creamy color and painting the doorways and windows and other trim a brownish, coffee-with-cream color. He was a nice, steady worker, I remember. He would move his ladder and his drop cloths around from place to place, and his big cans of paint, and just quietly paint and paint. Painted that whole library all by himself in just a week. Sometimes, at lunchtime, he and I would sit outside together to eat our sandwiches—we brought them with us from home—and we'd talk.

"He had an unusual accent. He came from someplace far away, and he spoke several different languages, so his accent when he spoke English was an exotic mixture of all the languages he'd spoken before he learned English."

"What did you and Mr. Damesek talk about?"

"Birds. We talked about birds. Mr. Damesek had a passion for birds. He was interested in every kind of bird and in every single thing about them. He even kept a pet parrot at home."

"And when did he paint the bird wall?"

"That happened on the last day. Late in the afternoon, when I was done, I came out of the children's room and, well, when I saw what he'd painted, I guess I was so surprised I must have cried out, made some sort of noise, and startled him. He was just finishing up, and he was lost in his work, completely absorbed in what he was doing."

"You startled him?"

"I did. He about jumped out of his skin. And he looked as if he'd been off on another planet. In some other world. He looked at me as if he'd never laid eyes on me before. It was that strange. And then he saw me staring at the wall he'd just painted . . ."

"And was that the bird wall, Mrs. Steiner?"

"It was the bird wall, Rachel. It was the wall covered with a flock of cream-and-brown-colored fantastical flying birds; beautiful imaginary birds.

"He saw me staring at the wall, and he stepped back and looked at it himself, and it was as if that was the first moment he realized what he'd been painting! Why, I believed then—and I believe now— he'd been painting it in a kind of trance.

" 'Don't worry, miss!' he cried—I was Miss, then, not Mrs.—'I'll paint over it! I did not know I was doing that! I never meant to paint birds on your wall. I'm sorry!'

"But I told him to leave it. I told him it wasn't *my* wall, but that I liked it, and I wanted to talk to the head librarian and the Library Board of Trustees about it. I told him he could always paint over it, but that I thought it might be nice for our library to have a bird mural in the entryway.

"He was reluctant to leave it, but I persuaded him. And then I persuaded the head librarian and the

Board of Trustees, too. Oh, I was crazy about that bird wall. And I was determined, in my quiet way, to keep it."

Mrs. Steiner stood very tall and looked proud, remembering. "Of course, the colors have faded over all these years," she said. "But I think the bird wall is still special, don't you, Rachel?"

"I do, Mrs. Steiner. I've always liked it. All the kids do. Except for some of the really little kids. Some of them are scared."

Mrs. Steiner laughed. "I know," she said. "But they get over it."

"Mr. Damesek is still alive, Mrs. Steiner," Rachel said, putting away her hose and the gardening gloves she'd been using. "Did you know that?"

"Still alive! My goodness, he must be incredibly old by now. I had no idea he was still alive. Are you sure?"

"I'm sure. I saw him the other day."

"Saw him? Where?"

"I saw him outside Mrs. Krnc's."

"I'm amazed," Mrs. Steiner said. "To hear that he's alive is surprising. To hear that he goes out is, well, astounding. He wasn't young when I knew him. And that's a long time ago."

"Did he ever paint any more of those murals, Mrs. Steiner?"

"He didn't, Rachel. He always seemed surprised that he'd ever painted anything but plain walls, even that one time. He said he didn't know what came over him. He was always rather apologetic about it. 'I'm just a housepainter,' he'd say, 'not an artist.' And I'd tell him, 'Even a housepainter can have a moment of artistic inspiration, Mr. Damesek.'

"I always hoped that once he retired from painting houses, he might take up painting birds, as a hobby."

"Maybe he did, Mrs. Steiner," Rachel said.

"Yes, maybe. Well, thanks for helping, Rachel, and for listening to that long story! I must be getting old myself, going on and on about things that happened such a long time ago."

"I love stories, Mrs. Steiner," Rachel said sincerely. "And I was especially interested in that one. Thanks for telling me."

Later that evening, after Rachel finished her homework and she and Uncle Benson were sharing a banana, yogurt, blood orange, Medjool date, and protein powder power shake, Rachel told him about her day.

"You took consonants to Mr. Gioia?" he said. "You two!"

"It was Brian's idea, Uncle Benson," she admitted, "and I didn't want to go. But we did find out some things."

"Like?"

"Like Mr. Gioia bakes the best lemon squares in the whole world."

"Better than mine?"

"Well, actually, yes."

"I see!"

"Not that much better, Uncle Benson. Just a little better."

"That's all right, Rachel. When I have time, I'll have to ask Mr. Gioia for his recipe." He cleared his throat. "Anything else?"

"He's bored."

"Mr. Gioia?"

"He hates being retired. He wants to work. He wants to be busy every minute. That's one reason he's taking such an active interest in the community, he said."

"Well, that *is* interesting, Rachel. I'm not sure how it could fit into a solution. But it feels like the kind of information that might somehow be useful. Anything else?"

"Well, something, I think something else. I was talking to Mrs. Steiner. And it turns out she knows, or rather she knew, Mr. Damesek. A long time ago. When he painted the bird mural. She was there in the library the day he actually painted it."

"Really? That must have been exciting!"

"But that's not what I want to tell you. What I want to tell you is that she told me Mr. Damesek speaks a lot of different languages. That he spoke a lot of different languages before he spoke English."

"And?"

"That's all."

Uncle Benson finished his power shake and wiped his mouth. "That's interesting, Rachel. And notice the pleasing balance of vowels and consonants in his name, if you would: Damesek. Four consonants. Three vowels."

"What does that have to do with anything, Uncle Benson?"

"Absolutely nothing, Rachel. I just thought it was interesting, since you and Brian have been so busy with vowels and consonants and names that are extreme in one way or another. I thought you might be interested in one that isn't. Good night."

11

On Sunday morning, Uncle Benson was up early, whistling and singing, banging around the kitchen as he prepared sourdough French bread French toast and Canadian bacon for everybody.

"Benson's International Breakfast," said Rachel's dad, pouring American Vermont maple syrup all over his food. "My favorite!"

It was Rachel's favorite breakfast, too, and she ate far more than she should have. "I can hardly move, Uncle Benson," she complained, mopping up the last bit of syrup on her plate with the last bite of French bread French toast.

"That's too bad, Rachel," he replied. "I was hoping you'd go over to Mr. Gioia's with me this morning. I'm supposed to meet with him at his house in fifteen minutes."

"You are?"

"I am."

"How come?"

"To discuss plans, Rachel, plans."

"Uncle Benson, you didn't tell me you had a plan! I'll be ready in a minute."

Rachel tore upstairs, brushed her teeth, and jumped into her clothes while Uncle Benson rinsed the syrup off the dishes and stacked them by the side of the sink. It was Lesley's turn to put them into the dishwasher and clean up the kitchen. But Lesley had disappeared right after she ate breakfast.

"She'll be back," Uncle Benson said. "She's somewhere around, talking on a telephone. I can hear her voice. Let's go. I don't want to be late."

Rachel listened. She couldn't hear Lesley's voice. But Uncle Benson was like her dad. He could hear everything.

They drove over to Mr. Gioia's in the grocery delivery van, and, before Rachel had time to worry about anything or to ask any questions, there she was in Mr. Gioia's spotless living room.

Uncle Benson admired the consonants on the mantel. Mr. Gioia smiled warmly at Rachel and thanked her for them again. They all sat down.

Rachel and Mr. Gioia looked at Uncle Benson and waited for him to speak. Uncle Benson cleared his throat and said nothing.

"Go ahead, Uncle Benson," Rachel encouraged, "tell Mr. Gioia your plan."

Uncle Benson took a deep breath. And said nothing.

"Out with it, Benson," said Mr. Gioia.

Uncle Benson sighed, leaned back on the sofa, and looked at his lap. "I don't exactly have a plan," he admitted.

"You don't?" said Rachel.

Uncle Benson shrugged sheepishly.

"But you said . . ."

"I said I'd think of one."

"Then what are we doing here?" Rachel asked.

"Yes, Benson," said Mr. Gioia, "then what are you doing here?"

Uncle Benson tried to rally. "Well," he said, "I decided to come anyway, even though I couldn't think of a new and better plan, because I thought—well, I thought if I gave you the new information, Greg, maybe *you'd* be able to come up with one."

"With one what?" asked Mr. Gioia.

"With a new and better plan."

"But, Uncle Benson, he likes the plan he has!"

"Well, he hasn't heard the new facts yet, Rachel."

Uncle Benson smiled weakly and looked at Mr. Gioia, who looked surprised, annoyed, and just a little bit interested.

Mr. Gioia cleared his throat. "So what are these new facts, Benson?" he asked.

"Well," said Uncle Benson, "now that I think about them, maybe they're not all that impressive. Maybe I've made too much out of them. Maybe I shouldn't be bothering you with them. Maybe they're not enough to make you even consider taking time to make a different plan . . ."

"Let me be the judge of that," said Mr. Gioia. "Pitch 'em to me."

"Mrs. Krnc *wants* to leave," Uncle Benson said. "Isn't that right, Rachel?"

"It is," said Rachel. "She wants to go hm."

"Hm?" Mr. Gioia inquired.

"I mean home, to her old home, far, far away. So you don't have to make her leave, Mr. Gioia," Rachel explained. "She *wants* to go."

"Then why hasn't she gone?"

"She hasn't got any money," Rachel explained.

"She can't go unless she has enough money to pay for the trip."

"And enough money to buy a little house for herself over there," added Uncle Benson.

"And enough money to live on, of course," added Mr. Gioia. "Yes, and?"

Rachel continued, "She hasn't got a real wig. Or any teeth. If she had money and a wig and some false teeth, she'd be happy to go. And nobody would have to send her to an old folks' home to get rid of her. Honest, Mr. Gioia."

Mr. Gioia frowned. He pushed up his sleeves. He rubbed his hands together and set them back on his knees.

"But this is all so simple!" he declared. "I can't believe you haven't thought of a plan, Benson."

"It is?" said Uncle Benson. "You can't?"

"It is. And I can't," Mr. Gioia repeated. "Why, look. The woman's house is worth quite a bit. Instead of having her removed from it because of her outlandish behavior and then selling it and using the proceeds to keep her in a home for old folks, we could just get her to sell it, and help her use the money to buy herself a wig and some teeth and a cottage, and a plane ticket . . ."

"Why, that's a terrific plan, Greg," Uncle Benson

said. "It's great. Simple and straightforward. Completely just and fair. And I think it would work, don't you, Rachel?"

"Somebody'd have to explain it to Mrs. Krnc," Rachel pointed out.

"That wouldn't be easy," said Uncle Benson.

"We'd have to find someone who speaks her language," said Mr. Gioia. "Or some language a lot like it." He shook his head. "There's a stumbling block."

They sat in silence, thinking.

"She's really good at pantomime," Rachel said. "We could try pantomime. That's how I found out she wanted to go hm, I mean, home, and that she needed money."

"Pantomime," said Mr. Gioia unenthusiastically.

Uncle Benson, too, looked unconvinced.

"Or maybe we could try Mr. Damesek," Rachel said. "Mrs. Steiner told me he speaks a lot of different languages. Maybe he speaks the pigeon lady's language."

"Mr. Damesek?" asked Mr. Gioia.

"The painter," Rachel explained. "The old man in the long black coat."

"The one I think painted a bird on my tarp?" asked Mr. Gioia. "Why—"

"Worth a try," said Uncle Benson, jumping in. "No harm in checking it out, eh, Greg?"

Mr. Gioia didn't answer right away. Rachel and Uncle Benson leaned forward and kept their eyes right on him.

He came around reluctantly, but he came around. "I guess it's worth a try," he finally agreed. "No harm in trying."

"But even if we can manage to communicate with Mrs. Krnc about selling her house," Rachel said, "I wonder who in the world will want to buy it?"

"It's in a nice neighborhood," Mr. Gioia pointed out. "It's on a lovely street."

"I've been inside that house, Mr. Gioia," Rachel said. "It's a mess."

"A mess?"

"I don't know quite how to describe it. It's just—a mess."

Mr. Gioia looked pleased. "Then maybe *I* could buy it," he said.

"You?" said Uncle Benson and Rachel.

"I could buy it and fix it up!" Mr. Gioia beamed at them.

"But, Greg, you're retired," Uncle Benson protested halfheartedly.

"And I hate being retired!" Mr. Gioia exclaimed.

"As I told the little lady and her friend the other day, I have never been so bored in my entire life as I have been since I retired!"

"So you wouldn't—um—*mind*—having a large, difficult project to work on?" asked Uncle Benson.

"Not *atall*, not *atall*," Mr. Gioia answered.

"There's only one thing," Benson continued. Rachel eyed him suspiciously. What was he up to now? "I'd thought about buying that house myself—"

"For what?" Rachel burst out.

"For a school," Uncle Benson answered. "For the school of my dreams, a place where students can come to be tutored instead of me traveling all over the place to tutor so many of them. I've even thought of a name for it." He looked away, as if he were reading something he saw written in large letters somewhere. "I'd call it The Guide on the Side Not the Sage on the Stage Learning Center: A Place of Joyful and Creative Learning for One and All."

"I can see it!" cried Mr. Gioia. "I can see it as if it were up in two-foot-high lights! I'll tell you what, Benson, *you* buy the place, and I'll help you fix it up."

"Why, Greg," Uncle Benson said, "that's a great idea. Then we'll both get what we need!"

Mr. Gioia looked very pleased with himself. "Just what I was thinking," he said. "*My* plan, exactly."

"I knew once you had all the facts, you'd come up with a great new plan, Greg," said Uncle Benson. "I congratulate you."

Uncle Benson agreed to contact Mr. Damesek. If he couldn't help, Mr. Gioia said he would find another translator—somewhere.

Rachel managed to keep her mouth shut until she and Uncle Benson got back into the van. Then she burst out, "Uncle Benson, you told me you had a plan. Then you told Mr. Gioia you didn't have a plan. But I think you really did have one. You just never said what it was. You let Mr. Gioia make a new plan. But you never said what *your* plan was!"

"*That* was my plan, Rachel," said Uncle Benson, smiling.

"What was?"

"For Mr. Gioia to come up with a plan."

"Uncle Benson!" she accused.

"Rachel!" he said, laughing.

On Monday after school, as Rachel and Brian and Lesley and Jonathan and Uncle Benson hurried down the hill from Twiddle's Fine Foods, they saw people standing around in front of the pigeon lady's house.

"Oh, no, Uncle Benson!" Rachel said. "I bet Mrs. Krnc's been out feeding pigeons. Mr. Gioia'll be mad all over again. Our new plan's sunk before we even get to try it."

Uncle Benson walked faster and didn't answer.

"Wait up," Brian said.

"Hurry up," Lesley scolded.

"Slow down," Jonathan argued.

They were all on edge as they approached the pigeon lady's house. But when they got closer, they saw that the people standing around weren't angry. Some of them were surprised and interested. Some were completely delighted. Mr. Gioia was already there. They were still too far away to hear what he was saying. But they could see him pointing, first toward the pigeon lady's house and then up the hill toward his parked car.

When they finally got to Mrs. Krnc's, here is what they found: out on the dilapidated front porch were Mr. Damesek and Mrs. Krnc. They sat on rickety chairs at a rickety table on which there were cups and saucers, a teapot, and a plate of cookies.

Behind them, the closed front door was spray-painted with fantastical flying birds! That old, weathered, paint-stripped eyesore of a door had been turned into a magical mural, as beautiful as the mural that graced the bird wall at the public library. And in front of it, the two old people sat happily drinking what Rachel knew was watery ginger tea and dunking what she knew were horrible spice cookies.

From time to time, they looked at the neighbors. Mr. Damesek tried to look fierce, but there was something impish about his expression now. And Mrs. Krnc could not hide her joy. When she spotted Rachel, she jumped to her feet, waved, pointed at the door and at Mr. Damesek, and put both hands over her heart.

Everyone understood that she was introducing the artist, and they clapped and cheered.

Mr. Damesek and Mrs. Krnc, it turned out, had two languages in common: Mr. Damesek spoke enough of Mrs. Krnc's native tongue to communicate in it. And then they had the language of love. For the two old people had, as Rachel's mom put it, "fallen for each other." It had been love at first sight!

So communication *could* take place through Mr. Damesek, and in the end, he and Mrs. Krnc decided that they both would be content living out the rest of their days together in her faraway home.

Mr. Gioia lost no time getting the new plan under way, and he did it with so much self-confidence that there was never any question in anyone's mind that the new plan really was far better than the old one had been. All the neighbors were relieved to be able to be positive and helpful, and nobody could quite remember how they could ever have thought they could have followed through on that other plan in the first place. "Things just got out of hand," one neighbor admitted.

"We never meant any harm," added another.

Mr. Gioia's efficient new committee communicated with Mrs. Krnc through Mr. Damesek. They helped her sell her house to Uncle Benson and (using pictures flashed across the miles onto Mr. Gioia's computer screen) buy a cottage just big enough for the two old people to live in.

Before anybody could say Jack Robinson, Mrs. Krnc had teeth, a wig, money enough, and several suitcases packed with all of her things. And she and Mr. Damesek (who had everything he wanted to take with him in the pockets of his coat and one large canvas bag) were on their way to the airport in a limousine hired for them by the neighbors, many of whom followed after in their cars in a long line, honking away. The festive procession was led by Mr. Gioia, who unwrapped his red sports car for the occasion. Lesley and Jonathan rode with him. Mr. Twiddle, Ling, Uncle Benson, Rachel, and Brian brought up the rear in the Twiddle's Fine Foods grocery delivery van.

So the pigeon lady got to go hm. Uncle Benson ended up with a falling-down house that had a marvelous mural painted on the front door.

And Mr. Gioia landed the fixer-upper job of his dreams.

"I never knew you wanted to have your own house, Uncle Benson," said Jonathan, making himself a snack with one hand and with the other holding open a large textbook he was trying to read.

"It's not so much that I wanted to have my own house, Jon. I wanted to have a place my students could all come to. I can work with so many more kids this way. And it'll be fun, too, to have my own tutoring center. Living there will just be an added convenience. It's not as if I haven't been happy living here, you know."

"That's good," Jonathan said, putting down his book to pay more attention to his snack. "Have you thought of a name for your—whatever it's going to be?"

"A learning center is the way I think of it. Well,

yes, actually, I have given some thought to what I'm going to call it. How does this sound to you, Jonathan?" Uncle Benson cleared his throat, as if he were about to recite a poem or give a speech. Jonathan stopped what he was doing to listen.

"I'm going to call it The Guide on the Side Not the Sage on the Stage Learning Center—"

"You are?" said Jonathan.

"Wait," said Uncle Benson, "there's more: The Guide on the Side Not the Sage on the Stage Learning Center: A Place of Joyful and Creative Learning for One and All!

"How does that strike you, Jon?"

"Long."

"Long?"

"Way long."

"Too long?"

"Way too long."

"Maybe I'd better think some more."

"I'd say so," said Jonathan. "After all, people have got to say it, kids have got to remember it. You don't have to put your whole educational philosophy into the name of the place, do you?"

"I guess not," said Uncle Benson. He didn't sound convinced. "What would you call it?"

Jonathan thought for a moment. "What's the address again?" he asked.

"826 Elm Avenue," said Uncle Benson.

"I'd just call it 826 Elm Avenue Tutoring Center, Uncle Benson. Everybody'll remember that."

"They'll end up just calling it '826 Elm,'" protested Uncle Benson. "Or maybe just '826.'"

"Yep," said Jonathan. "Nobody'll ever get lost trying to get there!"

"Everybody will remember it," Uncle Benson said quietly to himself. "Nobody will get lost trying to get there.

"Jonathan," he decided, "you're a genius! 826 Elm Avenue Tutoring Center it will be."

12

It took a while to get 826 Elm up and running.

Uncle Benson and Mr. Gioia made what seemed like endless trips to lumberyards and building supply centers, paint shops, hardware stores, electrical supply stores, and every other kind of place that sells stuff needed to fix an old wreck of a house.

But Uncle Benson was patient, and he was busy, too, and Mr. Gioia was the busiest, happiest man around.

Mr. Gioia made it look as if working on an old house was the most fun in the world. And soon many of the neighbors began taking a lively interest in what was happening at 826 Elm Avenue. Quite a few of them wanted to pitch in.

"It's the Tom Sawyer effect," Uncle Benson explained.

"What's that?" Brian asked.

"It's when Tom Sawyer has to paint a fence," Rachel explained, "and he doesn't like doing it, so he pretends it's the most fun in the whole world, so all the other kids want to try it. Right, Uncle Benson?"

"Right, Rachel."

"Then what?" asked Brian.

"Then everybody else paints and Tom Sawyer loafs around while they do his work for him."

"I don't get it," Brian said.

"What don't you get?"

"I don't get hardly—"

"I know that, Brian." Rachel rolled her eyes. "I meant, what don't you get about what I just told you?"

"I don't get what it has to do with Uncle Benson's house, and Mr. Gioia . . ."

"I can understand that, Rachel," said Uncle Benson. "It's not exactly the same thing. Mr. Gioia actually *is* having a terrific time and enjoying himself while he works on the house. He's not pretending. And all the neighbors want to participate because his enthusiasm is genuinely infectious."

"What's that?" asked Brian.

"Like a disease," said Rachel. "Catching."

"And that's the Tom Sawyer effect?" asked Brian. "Sort of like a cold?"

"Sort of," Rachel said.

"I'd say it *is*," Uncle Benson said firmly, putting an end to the conversation.

Early on a Saturday afternoon in June, Uncle Benson was finally getting ready to make the big move.

"I thought you'd stay here with us forever, Uncle Benson," Rachel said pensively as she watched him pack up his clothes and his books, his tennis racket and his golf clubs, his papers and his paraphernalia.

Uncle Benson stopped packing and sat down beside her on the guest couch that opened into a bed.

"It feels like the right time for me to have my own place," he said.

"I know."

"I won't be far away."

"I know."

"And you're welcome to come over any time you want to, Rachel, and to stay for as long as you like."

"I know."

"Things will be just fine. You'll see. You have nothing—absolutely nothing—to worry about."

"Everything will be different."

"Some things will be different," Uncle Benson agreed. "But some things won't be. You won't be different. I won't be different. We'll act the same. We'll feel the same. We'll love each other just as much."

"I know."

"You don't sound happy."

"I'm not happy, Uncle Benson. I wanted you to stay here with us forever. I got used to thinking you would. And now you're not. I don't want things to change."

"I understand," Uncle Benson said. And he stopped trying to persuade her.

They sat together on the couch for a while. The sunny afternoon was quiet. Someone down the block was hammering. Occasionally they heard a car go by. In the backyard, old Molly woofed in her sleep. The phone rang and rang, and stopped.

Rachel leaned against Uncle Benson, and he put his arm around her. She put her head against his chest and listened to the steady beating of his heart.

Finally she sat up.

"Better?" he asked.

Rachel nodded yes.

He smiled at her. Then he stood up and got back to work.

Rachel wandered off. She had end-of-the-year schoolwork to do, and then she was going to a sleep-

over at her friend Judith's house. She would stop in and see Uncle Benson at 826 as soon as she had time.

826 Elm Avenue Tutoring Center was a huge success. Nobody forgot the address, and everybody liked to come there. Uncle Benson's tutoring program included art projects, Pygmy math games, singing, dancing, cooking, and clowning—anything he could think of or anyone else could think of that would help children learn to be more confident readers, writers, thinkers, mathematicians, and all-around good citizens.

His results were good.

Teachers all over the district referred so many students to his school, he had to hire assistant tutors. And Mr. Gioia stayed busy keeping up with the wear and tear that active kids inflict on an old house.

In the fall, Rachel came by after school a couple of days a week to help the younger children make vowels and consonants out of colored Styrofoam and to help Mr. Gioia clean up the art room after the youngest students left and before the older ones came in the evening.

Uncle Benson sometimes fixed a quick dinner for the three of them during the break, and one evening, as they polished off the last of the Tuna Lorenzo

Casserole and the Green-as-Grass Green Salad, he produced an envelope with many colorful foreign stamps on the front.

"This came today," Uncle Benson said.

Mr. Gioia reached eagerly across the small table for the envelope, and Rachel got up and peered over his shoulder.

Inside was a color photograph of Mrs. Krnc and Mr. Damesek standing in front of their cottage.

Mrs. Krnc was wearing her new wig and smiling broadly, showing off her new teeth. Mr. Damesek had on black trousers and a white shirt and a black vest with fancy embroidery on it. He looked like a member of a dance troupe, just like the people in the picture Rachel and Brian had seen at Mrs. Krnc's that day.

Behind them was the door to their house, painted with cream-and-brown-colored fantastical flying birds. Propped over the door were the vowels Rachel and Brian had given Mrs. Krnc. And all around the happy old couple, milling about their feet, perched on their roof, and flapping in the air beside them, were pigeons.